CATARINA M.

The Depth
of Her Silence

ISBN: 978-1-971349-18-3

Introduction

Catarina's journey began in a quaint town of Monticello, Kentucky where the roots of her Southern charm and culinary prowess were firmly planted. At the age of four, she found herself under the wing of her grandmother, a culinary virtuoso celebrated throughout the town for her exceptional skills in the kitchen. With the guidance of her Aunt, she also found her passion for books, by being introduced to the public library. She absolutely fell in love with reading, especially mysteries and adventure.

Venturing into higher education, Catarina pursued her passion for communications and language at college, earning a degree in Journalism and Broadcasting. It was within this realm of writing that she discovered another avenue for self-expression and fell deeply in love with the art of storytelling.

Catarina's wanderlust led her to traverse the landscapes of Europe and America, immersing herself in diverse cultures and broadening her understanding of the world. Her affinity for both the written word and the culinary arts converged seamlessly when she embarked on the journey to publish her first cookbook, a culmination of her experiences, skills, and unwavering passion.

The second book was an anthology of transformative stories of Health and Wellness. This is her third book and it has a blend of passion for murder, mystery and love gone very bad. She enjoys the thrill of unraveling clues, hidden motives into unknown worlds of imagination.

Beyond her creative pursuits, Catarina cherishes the joys of life, finding profound fulfillment in her role as a mother. Driven by a desire to share her love for both writing and cooking, she seeks to inspire others to savor the richness of these experiences through the different genres she is able to write about. She continues to explore new creative paths, crafting many different stories of different types of genres.

Prologue

Sophie stood outside her car, staring out over the choppy waters of the Atlantic Ocean. She closed her eyes and took in the smell of the salt and sea. She was relieved to be leaving this place and wanted to put the events of the past few months behind her. She thought things would be different this time, a new place, a new start... but the last year had been a struggle. Too much of her past was trying to catch up with her. As Sophie reflected everything that went wrong, her instincts sharpen and her memories of the past resurface.

She quickly pulls herself together and takes a deep breath as she looks out over the ocean at the sunrise.

Even if moving forward might be worse than this, the longer I stay the greater the danger. The wind was beginning to blow harder and seagulls flew off into the distance. A storm was definitely coming, and even though it was barely autumn, Sophie felt a chill crawl up the back of her neck. This was always a sign that it was time to leave.

"Breathe" by Toni Braxton was playing on the radio as she sped away in her Mercedes. She caught a glimpse of the ocean in the rear-view mirror, and she thought of *him*.

Table of Contents

Chapter 1

One year earlier...

Sophie was new to this area, having been here only a few months. Well, it was another place where no one knew her, and she knew no one. She was walking to the reception area to call for the next patient when in walked a very handsome man that caught her eye. As he looked up, they locked eyes. It was as if they were the only two people in the room.

Sophie suddenly looked around and all eyes were on her. She stumbled to call the next patient. As Sophie took the patient to the room, she couldn't help but think about what had just happened. The man before, seeing him, had hit her in the head like a thunderbolt.

When it finally came to his turn, Sophie led the handsome stranger into the exam room and started asking him medical questions as she examined him.

Chad," he said.

Sophie jolted out of her daze. "What?"

"My name is Chad Thornton. You asked me my name."

Sophie's face turned red. "Oh, I apologize. It's been a long day already," she explained.

He smiled. "It's fine. I just came in to get my physical."

Sophie helped Chad with his appointment, and as she did, she learned about his military background and insurance coverage. She assured him everything was covered just fine. She explained that he was in very good physical health. She also told Chad she wanted to get labs on him so she could make sure he was as fit inside as he was on the outside.

Sophie blushed as she said that to him because he was most definitely in very fine physical health. She felt like she was about to have an orgasm thinking about it. Sophie pulled herself back to reality and realized that he was staring at her. She blushed even more as she told him where the lab was so he could get his blood taken.

* * *

Chad returned a week later to the medical office where Sophie was the head nurse. She looked up and was surprised to see him standing there. This man's eyes struck her with a kind of intelligence and seriousness - a powerful confidence that she couldn't ignore. A shocking and inexplicable heat poured through her as he held her gaze. His stare was bold, unflinching, as if he was accustomed to taking his fill of anything in his sights. That air of assumption should have offended her for many reasons, but as his mesmerizing blue eyes traveled the length of her, all she could feel was the rapid igniting of every cell in her body.

As he approached her, Sophie said, "Hi Chad. How are you?" He smiled, impressed that she remembered his name.

She said, "I make it a point to remember people's names, especially my patients. I associate something with their name, it makes it easier to remember their name and face."

He said, "Well, I guess you thought of the word 'cute' and remembered 'Chad' because both have a C." Sophie laughed very loud.

"That's pretty good," she said, "but it was your smile that I associated with you, it made me think of Candid Camera Chad."

Sophie asked, "How can I help you today, Chad?"

Chad took a deep breath and said "Well... that might be a great question for another day".

Chad told Sophie he wanted to check on the insurance coverage for his oldest son, since he would be going to college in the fall.

"The person at the front desk can answer your insurance questions," Sophie explained to him.

Then Chad admitted he was there because he wanted to ask her to lunch. Sophie responded quickly, "I don't date patients. Especially ones that have a wedding ring on."

Chad said, "Oh that's just for show and it's too tight on my finger. That's why I still wear it."

Sophie smiles, glancing at his left hand and then looks up at him again. Chad finally left.

* * *

Two weeks later, Chad returned to Sophie's office for the third time. When she looked up, eyebrows raised, she cocked her head to one side and said, "Let me guess, you're here, again, to be turned down?"

Chad smiled that gorgeous smile and shook his head. His eyes lit up when he smiled, and it was very hard for Sophie to not smile back. She had been thinking of him since the first time he walked into her office. Hell, she had even dreamed about him a few times. The dreams were steamy and left her sweating and breathing hard when she woke up.

As he approached her, she stopped daydreaming and looked at his gorgeous blue eyes.

He put his hands together and said, "I'm having some pain, and I need your medical opinion." He took her hand with both of his and placed it on his heart. "Can you feel it?? It's hurting bad. I think it's broken."

Sophie felt butterflies in her stomach. Her heart was beating out of her chest as he enclosed his fingers over hers. She smiled but couldn't speak.

Even though it was only seconds, it seemed like forever before she finally pulled her hand back and said, "Mr. Thornton, if you're having chest pains then I suggest you see a Cardiologist. Or I can call an ambulance and have you admitted to the hospital."

Chad's smile never changed. "Please let me take you to lunch sometime, nothing more, I promise. I would like to explain the ring, here's my phone number."

He put a piece of paper in her hand. Then turned and walked away.

Chapter 2

C had Thornton was a charmer, and he certainly knew how to smooth talk his way through anything. Sophie suspected that he could literally charm the pants off almost any woman, especially her. He knew exactly what to say and how to say it.

Chad was six foot one and towered over Sophie with his very fine physique. His look, demeanor, attitude and swag were the reasons she did a doubletake when he'd entered her office the first time. Chad's handsome Navy Veteran swag made their chemistry undeniable and intense.

Sophie Monroe was the kind of woman most people trusted - an exceptional nurse with a quiet presence, someone who keeps to herself. Though she is not a physically tall person, her blonde hair, beautiful brown eyes, and infectious smile made her appear strong and tall. But her lack of confidence in her personal emotions and love life made her a bit naive.

After going through a bitter divorce, she settled in Jacksonville, Florida to escape the pain of a toxic marriage and to try to rebuild her life. She's been here working at a huge medical facility for about 6 months now and things in her life were going well, she was finding solace, and her fresh start seemed to be falling into place. She actually felt like she can keep her secrets of the past buried this time.

If Sophie needed to stay away from a man like Chad Thornton, from *any* man in fact, she had plenty of reasons. But that didn't keep her pulse from speeding up as she watched him walk away. It didn't keep her heart from pounding and jumping every time she thought about his sharp blue eyes piercing through her and stripping her bare.

Sophie shook herself back to reality. *He is not for me. I know this.*

But every time she saw him, it didn't keep her from looking. She felt herself falling for him, but she knew she had to stop herself from doing that.

Again.

Sophie stayed focused on her objective: To be happy and focus on herself, by herself! *To handle yourself, use your head... to handle others, use your heart. Remember, the door to the human heart can be opened only from the inside.*

"So, don't judge me until you have walked a mile in my shoes," Sophie said to herself.

She intended to avoid (at all costs) the hot-as-sin, arrogant, but disturbingly arousing, Chad Thornton!

Sophie pushed the elevator button for her fifth floor apartment, wishing it was as easy to push the memory of those searing blue eyes out of her mind. But that man radiated a palpable heat and power that she could feel tripping up all her senses.

"He isn't my world. I need to remember that," Sophie said to herself. She knew she needed to put distance between them and kept hoping he would vanish, just like the secrets she carried.

But nothing ever truly vanishes.

As she let herself into the apartment, Sophie couldn't help but think back to the past, before she moved to Jacksonville. She tried to push those secrets deeper in her mind, wondered if she should have sought help for her pain. It wasn't a physical pain but an emotional one that hurt down to her heart and soul. Everyone should have someone to talk to, of course, but then someone else would know what was going on in her head.

Would know the secrets she carried.

It was hard for Sophie, in those early days in Jacksonville, to not have a support system. Judged by circumstances, haunted by the past. It had been many times that she had to take a leap of faith in her life. How else would she have lived with the circumstances she'd found herself in?

No. Sophie made her choices, got up, and walked out of hell many months ago. She kept moving, hoping the secrets wouldn't catch up with her.

Since Chad Thornton strolled into her life weeks ago, with his gorgeous smile, hypnotic blue eyes and a swagger that made her weak in the knees, she seemed to only wind up in her own head. Sophie decided she would be strong and start focusing on work and the things she loved to do. All the while, Sophie hoped and prayed that she wouldn't have to see Chad Thornton anymore.

Out of sight, out of mind, right?

* * *

Sophie spent the next several weeks working extra hours since they were so busy at her office with many sick patients. She realized that she had been too busy to think about Chad and was glad to not be thinking about him. However, she was getting frustrated with herself for thinking about it this much.

Oh damn!! Why is this starting again? she thought angrily. *I've had several months of calmness, relaxation in my life since I moved here. But now.... why did this man have to come into my office... into my life?* Sophie said to herself.

Yet there she was, thinking about those mesmerizing blue eyes that drew her in and made her so aroused. Sophie let herself fall into the daydream. Suddenly, it was like she could actually feel Chad's hands exploring her body. She went weak and moaned. Every emotion in her body responded to his touch as she felt an orgasm beginning to build in her...

There is a loud knock at her office door. Startled, back to reality, she catches her breath and opens the door.

The receptionist handed Sophie a vase full of beautiful flowers of all kinds. It also had sunflowers, her favorite. "These came for you a little earlier, Sophie," said Ella.

"Thank you, Ella" Sophie replied, and she smiled.

She sat back down at her desk and stared at the flowers and the card that was attached. Sophie had to make herself take a breath. She hadn't realized she'd been holding it. She was afraid to think about where the flowers may have come from. The last time she received flowers was before she moved to Jacksonville.

Fear rushed through her and she started shaking. Sophie wiped her face with her hands and told herself to get a grip. She opened the card and read it.

"You're such a lovely woman who deserves lovely flowers. I am mesmerized by your intelligence and bedside manner. I would like to take you to lunch... Please say yes." - From the man who has a reason to smile again.

Chapter 3

It had become one of their favorite places for a lunch rendezvous. Sophie loved Thai food as much as Chad did, one of the many things they had in common. Another reason it was their favorite, was the fact that it was across the road from the bungalow they had rented.

As they retreated to their little bungalow love nest, they could barely keep their hands off each other. Chad slowly started to undress Sophie, kissing her lips, cheeks, and neck. Sophie reached down to unzip his pants. She could feel the hardness between his legs.

She moaned and her legs started shaking. Chad removed her clothes and immediately ran his hands all over her and kissed her hard nipples. He caught her before she collapsed in his arms from the ecstasy she was beginning to feel as his hand slid between her legs into her soft, hot honeypot.

"Mmmmm, babe," Chad whispered. "I love touching and kissing you all over when you're naked. Can you feel how hard you are making me?"

"I want your kisses and tongue all over me," said Sophie as she cupped her breasts in her hands and held them while Chad was kissing them. He put her beautiful breasts in his mouth. Sophie almost screamed; could feel herself getting wet with anticipation of what Chad would do to make her have an orgasm. Many times.

Like he always did.

Chad slid his body between Sophie's legs and slowly pushed his hardness into her soft, wet, and oh so very tight vagina. Sophie let out a moan, then a little scream in ecstasy. Chad thrust harder and harder into her until they both came at the same time.

They both knew this lunch date would have to be shorter than usual. They were both expected back at their jobs.

But as they cuddled up in each other's arms, Chad said, "I just want to call and tell them I'm not feeling well and take the rest of the afternoon off. How about it, babe? Want to take the afternoon off and make each other very happy?"

"You have no idea how much I would love to have you inside of me for the rest of the day," Sophie said with a wide smile. "But I have to get back. There's a big meeting with the staff and the owners' of the medical office," she said sadly.

"Well, I think we definitely should take a day off very soon," Chad said excitedly. "I need a full day of you, our naked bodies, some food and drinks and maybe even some fun, erotic, kinky surprises."

Sophie turned and looked at Chad. "My body aches for you and wants that, too. The surprises sound intriguing. Even though I'm not a big fan of surprises most of the time!"

"Babe, I feel sure that you will like this one. Now kiss me hard one more time and then we can get out of bed before I decide to tie you to it and keep you here all day anyway," Chad laughed a bit of a demonic laugh as he pulled Sophie to him and kissed her very hard and lustfully. She saw a look in his eyes that was a bit frightening but tried not to let Chad see her scared.

Sophie loved it but was also a little disturbed at his laughter. She started getting dressed and wondered what it was Chad was thinking about and why she felt a little uneasy about his laugh.

Half an hour later, Sophie was having a difficult time paying attention at the office meeting. She kept thinking about her lunch date at the bungalow with Chad. She could still feel him thrusting in and out of her. But Sophie was also thinking about how Chad's demonic laugh made her feel uneasy.

They had been going to lunch and then finally started their wild and steamy affair for over a month now, but this was the first time she felt uneasy and unsure of Chad. That laugh and the hypnotic look in his eyes rather disturbed her.

A nurse tapped Sophie on the arm and told her to wake up. Sophie pulled herself out of her daydream and shook her head with a smile. When the meeting ended, Sophie went home and got settled into a hot, soapy bubble bath. Her bathroom was lit with candles and jazz music was playing on her sound system. She slid into the tub with a nice glass of Cabernet, and tried to get Chad's strange laugh out of her mind. She immersed herself in the bubbles up to her nose, turned off her thoughts, and soaked in the warmth of the water.

So that she could finally relax.

Chapter 4

Chad was home also, taking a shower after his afternoon at work. He started thinking about Sophie and their lunch rendezvous. He imagined every inch of her body and how he'd flicked his tongue over her nipples as he thrust himself inside of her, over and over, harder and faster.

Chad stroked his huge penis as he pictured all of that in his head. He moaned and then ejaculated in the shower, remembering their orgasms together in the bungalow. Then, Chad stepped out of the shower and walked into his bedroom, still wet.

"Well, well! Are you coming to bed soaking wet, my dear?" inquired his wife, Rosa.

He laughed and climbed into bed and immediately got on top of her and they began to have sex!! Very rough but stimulating, hard sex!!

Rosa Thornton was a strong-willed woman in her mid-forties who, in many ways, could be a real bitch. Rosa was pretty enough, but not at all what some would call striking or beautiful. She jumped from one meaningless job to another, never really feeling like she should have to work. She had used men in the past, and even her female friends, for money.

She and Chad had been married for over 20 years, during which time she had happily spent his hard-earned money as if he was a millionaire, instead of a retired Navy chief petty officer.

Rosa had always had affairs while married to Chad, because he was typically out on the ocean in a ship most of his time during his military career. So needless to say, Rosa was not the best role model for their two boys, and she never put their needs before her own. Chad was informed from one of his close friends that she had been having affairs with different men for a long time. So, he decided to retire after twenty-two years of service in the military, and that way he could be there for his boys.

Rosa's family lived close in the same area of Jacksonville as she and Chad. They were always conniving like Rosa, and therefore always encouraging her to do anything and everything to make herself happy. They convinced her that she should always be in control of everything, especially of Chad.

Rosa's Latino family were always putting Chad down and constantly in her ear about taking everything she could in order to live the life she wanted. So, Rosa was always using sex as a way to control Chad but still having sex with other men while Chad was working through the day.

Rosa made sure she still controlled the purse strings and convinced Chad that she should still take care of their budget and financial issues since she had done so while he was in the service and out to sea. She was spending money as she always had and was also pulling money to put in the account she opened only in her name. And again... she could be a real bitch!!

"That was a surprise," Rosa said, catching her breath. "I'm not complaining, mind you, but it was a definite surprise. Why are you so happy and aroused?"

"Why shouldn't I be?"

"I mean, most of the time you're tired or just quick to get your rocks off," Rosa hissed. "But I've noticed lately that you seem very different."

Chad just looked at her and said quietly, "I don't know. Maybe I'm going through *the change.*"

Rosa looked at him with a piercing gaze.

"You can be such an ass sometimes, Chad!" she yelled.

Chad laughed and went into the bathroom to wash Rosa's smell off.

Then he climbed back into bed. He smiled and closed his eyes as he thought about Sophie and her hot body, gorgeous eyes, and how he loved thrusting his hard penis into her wet, hot, tight special honeypot. He drifted off to sleep and dreamed of giving her many orgasms.

Chapter 5

Aweek had passed since Sophie and Chad had been to the bungalow. Sophie had been very busy at work and Chad had to go out of town for business, but she had been thinking a lot about him and their wild, crazy sexual encounters.

She thought back to a month earlier, when she had tried to convince herself not to get involved with anyone, especially Chad Thornton. But his charming, good looks and mesmerizing eyes had really won her over.

Suddenly her phone rang, and she smiled when she saw that it was Chad.

"Hello gorgeous man, I was just thinking about you," Sophie said in a sultry voice.

"Oh, were you now? I hope it was sexy thoughts of what you want me to do to you, my hot woman!" Chad said in his deep, sexy voice.

"Of course I was, and all the erotic things I want to do to you, too," gasped Sophie. "I have missed you baby, and your lips all over me… rocking my world."

"I missed you so much too, my sexy vixen. I am aching to touch you… kiss you. But you know, I couldn't just kiss you… I would have to undress you and make love to you," Chad said, breathing hard.

"I remember our last night at the bungalow. The next morning you left on your business trip," she said dreamily. "I need to see you very soon before I explode because yes, I'm *very* horny!"

"Oh babe, I remember that night like it was yesterday. You reached down, stroked my hard cock several times, then held on as you led me to the bed," Chad moaned into the phone.

"Are you still at your meetings?" asked Sophie.

"No, my love. I'm finally heading home. I must admit it's been a long week and I'm very tired," Chad said rather quietly.

"Well, I wish you were heading home to our love nest. I would be waiting for you naked, with a bottle of wine," Sophie said in her sexy voice.

"Oh, I would probably get a speeding ticket just trying to get there in a heartbeat. But I have to be at my son's baseball game early in the morning," he said sadly. "Cameron will be pitching and he's being watched by college recruiters for a scholarship," Chad said proudly.

"I understand, my sweet man. Enjoy time with your son and we will see each other soon I'm sure," she said.

"That's a promise, babe. I have so much passion built up in me," he laughed. "I will make you gasp and moan and orgasm over and over again!"

Sophie was getting hot and bothered just thinking about what Chad would do to her. She was so caught up in ecstasy, she forgot she was still at work.

"Chad my love, please get home safe and I hope you have sweet, erotic dreams about us," she said with a smile. "Good night you sex machine!"

"I will be careful and contact you soon. Good night my gorgeous, sexy woman," Chad said as he made a kissing noise through the phone.

Sophie took a deep breath as she hung up the phone. She finished her work, closed the office door, and headed home to her apartment. God, she missed that man. She suddenly realized that she might be falling in love. She felt a panic rush through her, and suddenly the past slipped into her thoughts again. Suddenly, Sophie wasn't sure she should be having feelings like this.

All she wanted to do was run and keep running. She's wasn't sure why she thought she could run away and these terrible things from her past wouldn't still be there. She tried shaking off these scary feelings and climbed into her bed all alone. As she drifted into a deep sleep she had thoughts of... *him*.

* * *

Sophie bolted up in bed, almost screaming, and breathed hard as sweat dripped from her face and hair. It took her a couple of minutes to realize where she was. She took a few deep breaths then gathered her thoughts. She hadn't had a nightmare like that for many months and, full of emotion, wondered why they had started again. She felt herself wanting to cry but immediately got out of bed and into the shower. She started talking to herself in order to distract her thoughts so that the nightmare could be buried deep in her brain. It worked, for now anyway, and she focused on her busy day ahead. Before she knew it, she was at work and focused on her patients and other staff.

Sophie's day went by fast, and for that she was grateful. She had only checked her phone a couple of times during her day, but there were no messages from Chad. Of course, she was a bit disappointed, but realized that her very busy day had occupied her mind and that was definitely a good thing.

While she finished catching up on her patients' files, there was a knock at her door. Two nurses from her staff wanted to let her know they were meeting a few more people from their office at a local pub.

"You should go with us and relax Sophie," said Angel, one of the nurses. "After all, it's Friday and it's been a really busy, stressful week."

Sophie definitely agreed about their busy week and decided to join them, so they left and walked to the pub together. She never really socialized much outside of work with anyone, except for Chad.

Sophie enjoyed her night out at the pub with her staff. She had a couple of margaritas, and when she looked up, one of the male nurses was bringing a tray of shots to the table. The shot glasses were filled with tequila, bourbon and vodka. She decided to do a tequila shot or two since it was her favorite, and was not a fan of bourbon or vodka. The next thing Sophie knew, she had more than a couple of tequila shots and Angel was helping her into an Uber.

* * *

Sophie slowly opened her eyes, she realized it was light outside. She looked at the clock and, when she was able to focus, saw that it said 10:10 in the morning. Her eyes widened as she sat up quickly. Panic set in because she thought she had overslept for work.

Then she realized it was Saturday, her head was pounding, and she felt nauseous.

"What the...? Oh yeah, tequila shots," she said aloud and she grabbed her head. "Why did I do that?"

She remembered she had not eaten anything last night either. She moaned and felt even sicker. She ate some crackers and cheese with some medicine for her headache and laid back down to sleep.

Music was playing.

Sophie opened her eyes and realized that it was her phone. It was Chad's ringtone.

"Hi baby," she said quietly, trying to wake up.

"Well, good morning sunshine. Or, I guess I should say Good Afternoon. You sound like I woke you up, are you alright?" Chad asked, sounding concerned.

"Yeah, but not really," said Sophie, who got herself out of bed. "I was asleep but it's ok. I'm so glad to hear your voice, sweet man."

"I had to get up very early this morning to get to my son's baseball tournament. We drove to the baseball stadium across the Georgia state line," Chad explained. "What's going on with you? It's after two o'clock in the afternoon and you're sleeping. Are you trying to catch up on some sleep from your busy week?"

"No not really," Sophie laughed. "I actually went to a pub after work yesterday with some of my staff and we had some drinks and a few tequila shots. I guess I forgot to eat anything too."

"Tequila?" Chad said in a surprised voice. "Oh my, can I do a body shot off you, babe? I really like tequila too!"

"I don't know, can you?" asked Sophie as she tried to laugh.

"Oh, I definitely can, babe. We will have a lot of fun," Chad said in a deep, dark voice. "Damn Sophie, you're so sexy and beautiful," he said as he was touching his hard cock.

Sophie felt very aroused even though she was still feeling hung over.

"It's nice to know you think I'm sexy, because it makes me want to have you right now baby," she said as she moaned into the phone.

"Oh, my sexy, hot woman you rock my world. I want to be inside your hot, wet honeypot right now with my hard cock," Chad said, and he too was moaning. "Oh, I must get myself back together, babe, since I'm at my son's ballgame. Thank God I'm in the restroom with a hard cock... and I'm about to explode."

"Well, that's too bad. You should be here with me so I could help you with that hard cock," Sophie said breathing hard into the phone. "I'm oh so very wet right now! I think I might need a spanking for talking like that."

"Babe, you're killing me right now. I got to go and 'release myself' before I go back out to the game." He could barely talk. "But a spanking you will get, very soon, you bad girl!"

Sophie let out a little laugh and she said, "Okay my sweet man, I'll stop. Just remember, that even though I'm a lady in the street, I'm a freak in the sheets with you. Laters baby."

She sat down on her couch and thought about Chad. She was truly falling for him. Every time she would think about it, it would upset her some because she would start thinking about things from the past and she did not want to go back in her mind to that time. She shook the feeling off. Chad was a good man, and maybe she was just getting too much into her own head.

After all, it had been many years ago since those things had happened. She wished she could just wipe it from her mind and pretend nothing ever happened.

Chapter 6

Weeks passed and Sophie had not let the thoughts of her life before Jacksonville creep into her mind. She had not had any more nightmares and was very happy and calm.

She and Chad spent many lunch dates and some evenings together at the bungalow making mad, passionate love. She felt as if they were falling very much in love and he had expressed to her how much he loved her, several times now.

Sophie felt so happy all the time now; her career was going wonderfully, and she truly loved her job and her staff at the medical center. Her love life was also a big part of her happiness, and she thought it was so different this time. But life and even love never goes perfect all the time, there are always hurdles, bumps and disappointments along the way.

Sophie was so excited for today.

It was almost noon, and she and Chad would be meeting up soon at their love nest. They had decided to take the rest of the day off from their jobs and spend a much-needed day together - and actually stay the night there, too. This would be the first time that they would stay all night together, and Sophie couldn't wait to be there and wake up next to him.

Chad ordered food to pick up from their favorite Thai restaurant across the road from their bungalow. She was bringing a bottle of their favorite tequila and some other food to have later. They arrived at the bungalow around the same time and could hardly keep their hands off each other. Lunch could wait. They were hungry for some dessert, first.

* * *

The bungalow backed up to a small dock and a lake. The water was beautiful and so serene that it made Sophie feel as if she was exactly where she was supposed to be. She never wanted to leave because this seemed to be her happy place, especially being there with the man she had fallen in love with. Chad slid his hands around Sophie's waist as she was looking out the window engrossed in the ripples of the water. She smiled and felt instant love from him as he brushed her hair back, his fingers lingering at her neck, then drawing her in for a kiss that was as seductive as their lovemaking.

After another round of wild, erotic sex, they finally decided they needed to eat some lunch so they could refuel their depleted bodies. They took their food out to the deck to sit by the water and enjoy their time there with each other.

Suddenly, the Florida sky changed from blue sky and sunshine, to dark clouds and strong winds, as Florida often does. A heavy thunderstorm rolled in and forced them to run back inside, laughing and getting soaked. Rain lashed against the windows, the air thick with the smell of wet bodies and Thai food.

Chad leaned against the kitchen counter, watching Sophie dry her hair with a towel. Lightning flashes illuminated her and he stepped closer, brushing damp strands from her cheek. Their lips meet, slow at first, then hard and deep as thunder rattled the walls.

Sophie jumped and screamed. Chad is surprised at first, and then he chuckles at her for being frightened by the storm. Sophie felt both safe, yet dangerously exposed, as if the storm outside mirrored the one inside of her.

One more thunder and lightning strike plunged the bungalow, and all the houses on the street, into darkness.

They looked at each other and said at the same time, "You get the candles, I'll get the wine." They laughed as Chad leaned over her and slowly kissed her neck.

In a low, rough voice he tells her he can't stop thinking about her. She smiles and their lips meet for a very passionate kiss as they fall onto the thick blankets on the floor.

They slowly undress each other. Chad climbs on top of Sophie, pushing her legs apart with his, and he thrusts his hard throbbing cock inside of her. Sophie lets out a little scream, but she feels ecstasy, too, as he pushes in and out of her fast and hard. He shoves his tongue into her mouth. He thrusts his tongue in and out to the rhythm of his cock's thrusts. Sophie opens her eyes very wide, shocked by the force of his tongue. But the ecstasy and orgasms are like being on the edge of a cliff... - thrilling but precarious.

After, they lay there breathing deep and smiling. Sophie looked at Chad. His eyes were closed, he had a strange smile on his face.

As she touched his cheek, Chad opened his eyes and said, "You make me so happy that I want to feel like this forever. You make me want to be a better person. I haven't stopped thinking about you since the first day we met.

"You've got this fire in you, Sophie," he continued. "Not everyone sees, but I do. I'd be a fool to ever let you walk out of my life, especially without telling you how much I'm falling in love with you."

Sophie sat up, looked at him, and she slowly smiled and said, "Baby I already knew I was falling in love with you before today. But hearing you say it to me out loud that you feel that way too, makes my heart pound very hard, because it's happy."

"I did not plan to come to Florida and find love. In fact, I kept fighting my feelings for you that kept trying to creep up when I first met you."

"As it's said, love finds you when you're not looking for it," Chad said as he caressed her face. "You are the sexiest, most intelligent, and best woman I've ever known."

"Well, I'm not sure everyone would agree with you about that but I'm happy to know that *you* think that way about me," Sophie said in a low, sexy voice.

She sat up again and said more seriously, "I would like to know something though. Why did it feel rough, and your kisses were a bit violent? You've never made love to me like that before."

"My sweet Sophie, I would never be violent with you. I'm sorry if it made you feel that way. I just get so passionate when I'm around you and it just makes me want all of you."

He put his hands on hers. "I thought you liked things a little Fifty Shades. I want to misbehave with you. So, I thought I would see if you were open to a little roughness, but I would never be violent with you, babe!"

Her heart told her that it was love, but her gut and instincts whispered that it was dangerous. But the heart wants what the heart wants, and she chose to ignore her gut.

"Chad my love, I would never think you would hurt me… not intentionally anyway," Sophie said lovingly.

"I think maybe we should talk about what we both want, and what works for us, before we get too rough. While I do like sex wild and erotic, and yes, even a little Fifty Shades, I draw the line at certain things."

"Oh babe, I agree that we need to make sure we're on the same page in every aspect of our relationship. I only want to please you, especially when it comes to making love," Chad said with a naughty smile and those hypnotizing eyes.

"But I'm being completely real with you on how much I love you. I haven't been able to stop thinking about you since the day we met."

He pulled her close to him. "I see you put on a brave face for the world sometimes. The perfect nurse, always reliable, always in control. But I see the real you Sophie, the one that carries around the weight of things no one else knows about."

Sophie looked at Chad with wide eyes, unsure what to say. Could he see into her mind, her soul? How could he know what secrets she'd pushed down so that no one would know?

"Baby, I'm not sure I know what you mean. For one thing, I'm definitely not perfect in any way," Sophie said very sternly.

"In the short time we've gotten to know each other, I don't see that you could know me enough to see my inner thoughts. But I do feel your love for me, and I want us to be able to make this relationship real because I have fallen hard for you," she said with a smile.

"Maybe we haven't known each other for very long, but it doesn't always take a long time when there's such a spark and attraction to each other as there has been with us since the beginning," Chad said and he kissed her hands. "I can see sometimes that you put on a brave, happy face, but you're not the only one who feels broken in places. I spent twenty-two years in uniform trying to be everything for everyone. A protector, a leader, everyone's rock. All it did was teach me how to hide the pieces that cracked underneath. But when I look at you... somehow, it doesn't feel like I have to hide anymore."

A big smile came across Chad's face and he continued. "Sometimes you're not easy to love... Hell, you challenge me in ways no one ever has.

You're real, you're brave, except in thunderstorms." Sophie punched his arm and he laughed out loud. "And you're so beautiful in every way. So, here I am. No games, no mask. Just a man who's made his share of mistakes, in front of the one thing in this world that feels right."

Her eyes locked onto his.

"Let me in, Sophie. Let me prove I'm not like others who might have used you or hurt you, because I can tell someone has. I'm not going anywhere, Sophie. I love you!"

He kissed her softly and sensually. She kisses him back, and put her arms around his neck , their tongues playing in a dance of love. Sophie felt his love all around her, and she actually feels safe.

When the kiss ended, she smiled at Chad and caressed his cheek. "My sweet man, you have made my heart swell with so much love that it's beating out of my chest," she said and grabbed his face with both hands.

She kissed his mouth and her tongue dipped inside, searching for his. This excited Chad and his hands moved to touch and squeeze every part of her body.

Sophie started to moan louder and louder as his hands grabbed her between her legs. His fingers were inside her now, and she started rocking in rhythm with his body and fingers.

Chad got her to her first orgasm quickly. Then he pulled his fingers out and immediately thrust his hard, pulsing penis inside her so that he could still feel her orgasm. Sophie screamed in ecstasy, and she wrapped her legs around his body so she could pull him harder and deeper inside of her. They moaned and rocked as they kissed each other deeply. Their passion was real and provocative as they fuck each other very hard.

They move to different positions, and finally climax together when Chad takes her from behind. They fall over onto the pile of blankets, sweaty and breathing so hard that they couldn't say a word.

Chapter 7

As Sophie slowly opened her eyes, she looked around and realized it was dark outside. She sat up and looked at Chad, who was sleeping and snoring a little. She shook her head, trying to wake up, and she grabbed her phone. It's was after 8pm and Sophie smiled, because she couldn't believe they'd fallen asleep for a few hours. Their love fest apparently wore them out. She quietly got up from the floor and realized she was in need of a bottle of water. As she closed the refrigerator door, she jumped with a little squeal as she saw Chad sitting up.

"OH! You startled me baby," Sophie giggled.

Chad laughed and he got up from the floor. "Oh, my legs are shaking and a little sore. You knocked me right out you hot, sexy, woman and I still want more of you. It feels like we slept for hours."

"We did, lover man. We climaxed together and fell asleep together," Sophie said lovingly. "I can't think of anything better that I would rather be doing!"

"The same for me my love," Chad said, and he took the bottle of water from her and gulped half of it down. "Ahhh... I need my electrolytes to get my strength back so we can do that again and again!"

He grabbed Sophie and they laughed and kissed.

Then, Chad pulled back and with a surprised face and said, "Babe, do you realize we get to have this entire night together and then watch the sun come up on the water in the morning? I am so happy and so very blessed that you are in my life. I can't wait to make love to you all night and give you all the orgasms you want, my love."

Sophie smiled and took a deep breath and said, "Nothing would make me happier, baby... it's the best blessing that we finally get to spend the entire night together and wake up in each other's arms. To see the sun rise with you is a dream come true."

They kissed and held each other for a few minutes, then Sophie looked at Chad lovingly and said, "Baby your kisses are so tasty but if we don't eat some real food now... I might have to take a bite out of *you*!"

She laughed very loudly and he smacked her bare bum and he said, "Oh yeah? I might take a big bite out of that bare bum, you gorgeous naked woman!"

Sophie started getting some food prepared for her and Chad as he prepared some steaks to throw on the grill. They laughed and talked as they worked together on their meal. Sophie felt like she was in heaven and so very much in love, she started thinking how wonderful it would be if they could stay like this forever.

Chad said, "Babe did you hear me? Where did you go? Looked like you were a thousand miles away."

Sophie looked at Chad with a startled look.

"Huh? Oh, sorry sweet man, I was just daydreaming about us being here in our paradise together," she said, and smiled. "What did you say?"

Chad laughed out loud. "I asked you if you could make us some Margaritas since you're a better bartender... I want to drink some tequila with my steak and then maybe some tequila body shots for dessert, my sexy gorgeous woman?"

"Oh, baby that sounds like a fantastic idea… margaritas and steak! Tequila body shots for dessert? I'm all in for that!" Sophie wiggled her eyebrows up and down. She turned, grabbed him around his waist, pulled him towards her, and kissed him passionately.

"Mmmm, my love. Your kiss is like candy… I can't get enough. But you are making me hard and if we don't stop now, we'll never get anything to eat… except each other," Chad said. "Make us some margaritas, my sexy wench!"

He grabbed her bootie hard with both hands. "I definitely want to have my tequila body shots on you the rest of the night and make you moan so loud. I might even have to spank you because I know you have been a naughty girl!"

Chapter 8

As Sophie slowly opened her eyes, she realized it must have been early. The sun was just coming up over the water behind the bungalow. Suddenly, a big dark shadow blocked her view of the sunrise. As her eyes opened wider, she realized Chad was standing over her - naked - with two cups of coffee in his hand.

"Good morning, babe... you look so sexy when you wake up! I could really get used to this view every morning," he said, smiling devilishly with his blue eyes glued on her. Sophie stared deep into those hypnotic eyes when Chad broke her trance, putting the cup of coffee in front of her.

"Here babe, I think you need this. Let's step out back and watch the sunrise like we planned," he said.

The sky was still blushing with the first light of morning, streaks of rose and gold spilled across the water behind their bungalow. The waves whispered against the shore, soft and steady, as though the world itself was quietly waiting. Sophie and Chad were wrapped in a warm blanket where they sat on the bungalow's porch swing. She leaned against Chad with her tangled hair from the night before. Chad didn't mind her crazy hair. He put his arm around her and pulled her close enough to feel the warmth from his naked body.

For the first time since their secret relationship had begun, words, not touches, filled the air. They began to truly talk to each other and watched the sun peek over the horizon as it slowly appeared to climb through the sky.

Chad turned to Sophie, opening up about regrets that he rarely spoke to anyone about. He told her about the weight of choices he carried from his Navy years, the fear of being seen by others as less than the man everyone believed him to be. Sophie listened as she focused on what Chad was saying but she also thought of her own choices from her past. She decided her secrets needed to stay buried, she wasn't ready to share the fragile pieces of guilt she carried. She returned her focus to Chad as he was finishing his confession.

"I want to be a better person... you make me want to be better, my lovely Sophie!" Chad said and kissed her hand softly. "You are so beautiful, you are the reason I smile all the time now. You will be in my heart forever. You are the only one that I've ever opened up to about these things from my past. I want to spend the rest of my life with you, my love, that's why I wanted you to know about my fears."

Sophie leaned over and very affectionately kissed Chad on the lips, which he reciprocated with an open mouth kiss. She slowly smiled as she sat up straighter to look at him.

"I knew something hit me straight on the forehead the first day you walked into my office," she said. "I tried hard to keep you at arm's length, denying what I felt was happening. I stopped fighting it realizing how happy and tingly I would get when I would see you... even just thinking about you."

"I felt the same hit in the head, babe, the day I walked in. You looked up, and our eyes locked, and we couldn't look away," he said and grinned.

"I do want you to know how special I feel that you trust me enough to share your fears. I will always listen and be here for whatever you need.

I love you," Sophie said and she put his hand on her heart. "I too have fears at times, mostly from bad dreams. But when I wake up the next morning, I tell myself it's another day and I don't think about it anymore."

"Well babe, did you have bad dreams last night?" he asked.

"No, I didn't. I slept like a baby," she admitted happily.

"Ok then, it seems that we make each other happy and relaxed sleeping together," Chad said. "You didn't respond when I told you how I feel about wanting to be with you forever. So, can you tell me the same?"

Sophie sat back and said, "Can you answer a question for me first? Are you still married?"

Chapter 9

Chad looked at Sophie with a sobering look on his face.

As he stood up, he stumbled for words, then suddenly, almost shouting, he said, "Babe, I love you so much and everything I've said is true... except... I wasn't completely honest about my living arrangements."

Sophie looked up at him and felt the emotion draining from her heart. She felt conflicted, vulnerable... maybe even naive. She started remembering why she didn't trust easily. Sophie sensed he was holding something back - the truth he did not reveal to her about his marriage.

"Are you going to answer my question... truthfully?" she asked him in a bit of an angry tone.

Chad looked like a kid caught with his hand in the cookie jar. He answered with a quiet voice, "I am still married as of right now. I am taking steps to see how to get the divorce without it ruining me financially. Finances have been the big key, also I'm trying to work things out so that my boys won't hate me. I told *her* I wasn't happy, and we need to get our finances in order. She wouldn't tell me much, she's always taken care of the finances. I don't have a clue what she's done with all the money that I made while I was in the Navy and out to sea," Chad kept explaining.

"I did actually leave for a couple of days right after I told her I wasn't happy... but I came back."

Sophie was halfway back inside the bungalow by now; Chad talked and followed behind her. She gave a bitter half-laugh and her eyes were piercing through him.

"You're *still* married, *and* you moved back in with her, so that's the way it is?" she asked angrily. "I broke my rule of dating a married man. I knew this would not turn out good, but I let you pull me into your life and then started falling in love... Talk about naivete! I'm so pissed at you right now but even more with myself!"

"Sophie please don't be upset, I'm sorry I wasn't honest with you. I am trying to get this divorce taken care of... I was afraid that if I told you that I had moved back home, then you would not want to be with me anymore," Chad said sadly. "There's so many parts to this divorce that I have to make sure it gets done correctly... military participation as well as everything else that goes along with a divorce."

"You say you're making good money now with this government contractor job, so you should be able to start taking control of your finances. You are the only one that can make your life better," Sophie said sternly.

"I'm not trying to tell you how to handle your affairs with *her*, I'm just saying that I've been through divorce with kids and finances involved. If you want out badly enough, you will work it out."

Chad moved toward Sophie and cupped her cheek in his hand and he said, "I know you're hurting and I'm the reason. Babe I'm really sorry."

He took her by the hands and they sat down on the bed. "Please know that we *do not* sleep together. I stay in the guest bedroom. We are living as roommates right now until I can get things set to move out and move on. I only love you babe, I only want you... You are my everything.

I really hope that you and I can move on together. Is that possible? Can you forgive me, please?"

A heavy silence hung in the air when Sophie stood up, staring at him for what seemed like an eternity to Chad.

Quietly, almost to herself she said, "God you're good. You sit there, so charming with the broken pieces of life, saying all the right things, like you've been rehearsing it for a while. Hell... maybe you did! You're obviously a man who knows how to get inside a woman's head... among her other parts... and make her heart forget what her gut is screaming."

Chad stood up beside her and started to say something, but Sophie put her hand up. He closed his mouth and lowered his head.

Her voice was still soft but gaining strength when she said, "You want the truth, Chad? You scare me. Not because I don't feel something... I *do*. That's the problem. The feelings are there! This pull towards you, I don't understand it... and I don't fully trust it.

Sophie took a few steps as she said, "You know, I've been here before, with a different face... a different voice... yet the same story. Like you, he saw me. He got me. He made me feel like I was finally safe to fall. And then he was..." her voice cracked slightly. "I'm not that woman anymore."

She took a breath and looked away for a few seconds, then back at him. "Damn you for making me want to believe," she yelled and she ran into the bathroom, slamming the door.

Chad, now dressed in his jeans and T-shirt, was in the kitchen getting another cup of coffee. He turned around when Sophie came out of the bathroom, wet from her shower. She immediately stepped into the bedroom without looking at him and got dressed quickly.

Chad walked over to her, but before he could say a word, Sophie turned to him and said, "You say you're not like the others. Fine... Then don't say another word about love. Maybe with time you will be able to show me the truth about you."

Chad looked at her with sadness and some fear in his face.

"I hope you know how I feel, but you told me not to talk about love," he said quietly. "I can't take it if you leave me... I will show you how truthful I am. I want your trust and love, so please tell me you will let me prove it to you... Don't run away from me babe."

Sophie brushed past him with her bag and purse in hand as she headed outside to her car. Before getting in, she turned and looked at him one last time.

"Looks like our first sleepover didn't quite turn out like either of us thought it would. This was your shot, Chad!"

As Sophie opened her car door, she said, "Look... I'm not saying yes but I'm not saying no either. Because if you're lying... if this is some twisted game... I can promise you, I won't be the one who ends up hurt!"

Chad just looked at her very sadly as she sped away.

Chapter 10

The alarm blared and Sophie rolled over to turn it off. She stared at the ceiling and she realized it was Monday morning.

Back to the office, she thought. At least her busy week ahead would keep her mind busy, as well as physically. She closed her eyes and she thought about the erotic and beautiful night with Chad at their bungalow. How could one question turn it into a nightmare? How could he still be married to her?

And he even moved back in there too, she thought. Realizing she was going to be late, she hurried to get herself ready for work and decided to grab coffee and a bagel on the way to work.

The week went by fast, and Sophie was glad it was Friday when she drove to work that day. She had switched her phone to silent mode for most of the week, so she didn't have to hear the texts from Chad on her phone.

He even dared to call a couple of times, as if she would have taken his call.

She really just wanted to be left alone for now. Everything that had happened was bringing all the old horrible thoughts and feelings to her again. Sophie felt the situations were much the same... she knew this is why the past was trying to creep up again. She turned up the radio louder as she tried to push those thoughts out of her mind... as if that really works.

Sophie was having a hard time focusing all through the morning. Every chart she went over, every client file she input into the computer would not keep her mind occupied. When it was almost lunch time, Sophie decided to go out and grab some Thai food. As she pulled into the restaurant, she looked across the street and saw their bungalow love nest. Her emotions were suddenly all over the place as she thought about the weekend before. She remembered it started out so positive and filled with love and hope...

Before she knew it, she walked into their bungalow.

She stopped and took a deep breath... *It still smells like us.*

Coffee, salt air and that mix of passion... then heartache. She replayed the weekend in her head - how his smile disarmed her, how his kisses made her forget the world. Her thoughts changed when she heard the echo of her own voice, raised, accusing Chad and doubting him... She felt that old ache rise back up in her heart. She didn't know if she was chasing love or repeating mistakes that she swore she'd never make again... Who knew? Maybe both? All Sophie knew was that this man had carved himself into her in a way she couldn't seem to wash away. And that terrified her almost as much as her past did!

All of a sudden, she was shocked into reality as she turned to see the door opening.

Chad stood there, looking at her with those gorgeous, mesmerizing eyes. He forced a grin and said, "Guess great minds think alike!"

In the silence, their argument from the weekend felt like ghosts still clinging to the walls. The shock of seeing him there was both comforting and suffocating, too. The air between them was heavy, neither quite ready to admit that they both couldn't stay away.

He smirked , trying to mask his own surprise. "Didn't think you'd come back here so soon... but it makes my heart so happy that you're here. I wanted Thai for lunch and was surprised and excited when I saw your car in the parking lot. I came over here wondering... actually hoping you were here... and you are!"

Sophie's pulse raced... she did not expect to run into him here. She stepped back too quickly, banging into the counter as Chad stepped towards her, but neither spoke, because words would only cheapen the electric current threading between them. Chad stood in front of her, blocking the way as Sophie tried to get past him. His gaze dropped briefly to her lips, and she bit her bottom lip. Then his gaze flicks back to her beautiful eyes. Sophie can't shake the sense that this is less about her and more about control.

"Are you going to keep pretending none of this happened?" he asked, voice low and rough. Her breath hitched , torn between escape and surrender.

She moved away from him and said rather angrily, "It was supposed to be perfect. Our little love nest escape... just you and me, tucked away where the world couldn't find us. For a while, it felt like I was living a dream... your mesmerizing eyes, your smile and laughter, the way you looked at me like nothing else mattered. I wanted to stay in that moment forever."

She took a deep breath and calmed down. "But the serenity didn't last, did it? I asked one question and suddenly the dream cracked. How can love burn so hot one night, and feel so cold the next morning? I keep asking myself if it's just passion... fire always has sparks, but deep down... I'm afraid of the flames."

Chad looked at her, scared that he was going to lose her. "Sophie, I want to hold you so very much and make you feel safe and loved... but I know you don't want me touching you right now even though I feel both of us are dying inside. I want you... no, I NEED you. I know you still love me because I can feel it, my beautiful woman."

Sophie immediately cut him off.

"I don't understand you, Chad. One minute you held me like I was the only woman in the world... and the next you cut into my heart with the words... that you were still married and had moved back in with *her!* Did you know how hard it was to open my heart? To trust again after everything I'd gone through in the past?" she asked and she could feel herself tearing up.

"And I let you in, and maybe that was my mistake. But if love with you meant walking on eggshells, waiting for the next storm, then... What the hell was I doing? You might think I was a fragile female... well I wasn't! I could stand on my own. Even though I thought I wanted to stand beside you."

Chad moved towards her as he took her hands in his and said in a begging voice, "Please tell me you aren't done with us... I couldn't stop, because I still love you as I always have. I wanted a chance to prove how much I did. This had been the longest week I could remember... my heart has never hurt this much in my life."

Sophie pulled her hands back rather quickly and she moved away from him.

"I wasn't going to say that I didn't believe you... because everyone has their own feelings about something or someone. But I wasn't sure you really knew whose heart hurt the most," she said hurtfully. "I knew how I felt, and that's why I was ready to think about a loving future with you... maybe even forever. But maybe the timing wasn't right, because it felt like you took a knife, plunged it in my heart and even twisted it for effect after you finally admitted you were still married and had moved back in with her."

"It was so hard to believe you after you lied to me about this... I just don't understand you, Chad, except that I was just another notch on your bedpost... so to speak," Sophie said as tears started forming in her eyes.

She immediately started walking fast toward the door, not letting Chad say another word to her. He rushed out the door behind her and she stopped in the driveway, a battlefield of unspoken tension.

She put up her hand and loudly said, "STOP! I don't want to hear anything more from you right now... I just can't do this, please give me space and time!"

She ran across the street and started to cry and slammed the door of her car. Looking in the rearview mirror she saw him standing at the edge of the driveway. She stayed in the car, gripped the wheel and debated whether she should drive off or throw it into reverse and floor it.

But she took a deep breath and said to herself, *Just leave... don't do this again, you know what will happen!*

* * *

Sophie drove straight home and called her assistant to cancel her afternoon appointments, saying that she had eaten something bad for lunch and was feeling nauseous. She actually did feel nauseous from her encounter with Chad, so she wasn't really lying. She was more upset than she realized, but her nausea reminded her that she needed to eat something, as she had not eaten since the night before. After, she snuggled up with a blanket on her couch and decided to read a book to take her mind off Chad and their terrible confrontation. Before long she dozed off into a deep sleep.

"YOU'RE A LIAR! How could you do this," shouted Sophie when she woke up suddenly.

Her hair and face were wet with sweat. She sat up, breathing very hard. Shaken and even frightened, it was one of the worst nightmares she'd had in a long time.

Sophie stood up and glanced out her balcony door to see that it was almost dark. She began to calm down as she poured herself a glass of wine. Then she sat back down with her glass to watch a movie so that she could get her mind off the nightmare. She even had another glass or two to self-medicate the anxieties of the day, but it didn't seem to be accomplishing more than just a good buzz.

Chapter 11

Sophie barely slept that night. After her unexpected meeting with Chad, and the nightmare, she was once again reminded that the past and her secret would always be there. Every time that she closed her eyes, she saw Chad at the bungalow. His words still clung to her skin like smoke, leaving her with a mixture of hurt and anger. She felt very restless and unsettled because, even though he didn't know everything about her. The thought of him uncovering the pieces about her that she has kept so carefully buried sent a shiver through her chest. Sophie finally got out of bed, she knew it was a lost cause trying to sleep, and it was breaking dawn anyway.

As the day went flying by, she busied herself with cleaning, laundry, and even a little trip to the grocery store. Sophie was cooking her favorite pasta dish for dinner - Chinese long noodles with shrimp, along with a glass of her favorite Cabernet. She loved to cook when she had the time, it always seemed to relieve stress, but today was not one of those times.

Seeing Chad the day before had shaken that illusion of relieving her stress. He had a way of stirring things in her, not just desire or even anger, but memory, too. Too many memories about certain things and mistakes that she could never undo. Chad only brought back those memories that she had tried so hard to forget... yet she could hear the voices echoing about secrets whispered in the dark.

* * *

By the time Monday came around, Sophie carried her smile at work like a fragile mask. Her patients adored her, the other doctors and her staff respected her, and had no reason to suspect the storm that churned beneath her calm surface. Yet every kind word she said felt like a lie because of the shadows she carried inside.

It had been almost a year since she allowed herself to think about what happened... since she'd forced herself to believe that silence could keep the past from clawing its way back into the present. But since she had let Chad into her life, she was frightened that everything was floating to the top of her brain uncontrollably. She found herself replaying her argument with him, and all the voices and their secrets, in her mind.

She felt anxious again as a deeper fear gnawed at her. What if Chad really did find out about her past? What if he uncovered the truth, and even worse... tried to use it against her? The thought that she had been trying to carefully build a new life for herself and that it could crumble apart... that was unbearable! She felt the panic try to set it in, and her breathing increased.

She immediately started her breathing technique in order to calm down and it definitely helped. She decided to avoid going by the bungalow and the Thai restaurant so she could avoid seeing Chad again. She started feeling calmer and told herself that would be the best idea, in order to avoid the panic she had felt a few minutes ago.

The night was long again. Lying awake in the quiet of her apartment she caught herself whispering a prayer she hadn't spoken in years. As if

God himself might somehow erase the sins she carried. Still, deep down she knew there was no erasing, no undoing. The past is always there, like a cruel demon waiting for the wrong moment to surface. She wanted to blame everything on Chad. After all, everything was resurfacing now. And at that moment Sophie told herself she hated him, but in reality, she knew the secrets of her past were her own doing and if she didn't pull herself together, it might be her own downfall.

She could not let that happen.

Chapter 12

By the end of the week, Sophie's reflection in the mirror looked almost like a stranger to her. A nurse practitioner in crisp scrubs, hair pulled back neatly, with a smile painted on her face, was the woman everyone else saw. But behind her eyes lurked the female who had made choices that she could never confess, the woman who lived with ghosts that she dared not name. And now that Chad had come into her life, she wasn't sure how much longer she could keep the two versions of herself from colliding.

Why were all these secrets from the past trying to drive her insane? Was it a warning that something evil was about to show up in her life?

The next night, Sophie stood on the balcony of her apartment and watched the Jacksonville lights glitter against the background of the city. She wondered if Chad was out there, perhaps thinking of her too. He had done what she asked and had not contacted her since their argument. A reckless part of her longed to call him... to hear his voice again and end this aching silence.

But her hand froze every time she reached for her phone, because she knew better than to open that door again. She wasn't sure she *should* open that door again since she had felt that undeniable danger. Chad wasn't just a temptation... he could be that risk she should possibly avoid.

Yet her body betrayed her, remembering every touch of his hands, lips and body, as if her heart wanted her to surrender. Sophie could almost imagine him standing there on her balcony, staring at her with his gorgeous hypnotic eyes, until she confessed every sin she had had hidden.

The thought both terrified her and sent an ache through her that she couldn't admit, even to herself. Sophie knew that this battle wasn't over. Was she lusting for someone she can't trust and the best thing to do would be to walk away?

But she can't control the urges or passion for him. What she didn't know, what terrified her the most, was whether Chad would be her salvation, or the man who would destroy her.

She warned herself that he was a man who could break her heart or even expose her secrets and leave her with nothing but ashes. But the woman in her had tasted the way he kissed, had felt his arms wrapped around her and had especially felt the passion of their endless lovemaking. She craved him with a desperation that made her feel weak.

But weakness was something she had sworn to never allow again. She finally said goodnight to the flickering lights and fell asleep, hoping the week ahead would be better and much calmer for her.

* * *

Each day she tried to throw herself into work, tending to patients who needed her steady, calm presence. Yet behind every smile and soothing word lurked a restless undercurrent. Her mind would drift to thoughts of Chad. The sudden softness of his voice when he let his guard down, his mesmerizing blue eyes, and gorgeous smile. She could feel the heat between them that refused to die no matter how badly they had hurt each other.

He was inescapable, even when he wasn't there.

By the end of another week, Sophie had not heard anything from Chad, and she realized the pain she was feeling was from her heart. She wondered if he had given up on their love or maybe he had just been playing her all along.

"I guess it was easier to stay married to *her*," she said to herself in a jealous tone.

She tried to get back to working on her computer and her clients' files, to push him out of her thoughts. Eventually, her office phone buzzed, and her assistant informed her that there was an unscheduled patient in the waiting room insisting on seeing her.

"His name is Chad Thornton," she said.

Sophie's heart raced, and she stood up as Chad walked into her office. He said thank you to her assistant and she closed the door behind her.

Chad looked into Sophie's eyes, smiled and said, "Hello, beautiful."

Sophie gave a half smile and said hello back, trying not to show that her heart was doing flip flops. She told him that he could have a seat, but he said he would rather stand because he wanted to tell her that he had been doing a lot of thinking.

Sophie took a deep breath and said, "Okay, I'm listening."

"I want you to know that I spent most of these last few weeks soul searching. I've been stubborn and I've been proud, but none of it means more to me than you do."

He sounded truthful.

"I know I hurt you and I hate myself for it," he continued. "You're the best damn thing that's happened to me since my kids were born, and I'd be a fool to let my pride take that away. I don't need to be right, and

I don't want to fight anymore. What I need is you beside me, even when life feels like it's falling apart. I love you, Sophie Monroe, and if you'll please let me, I'll spend the rest of my days proving it to you. Will you let me back in so we can at least talk?"

He looked at her with begging eyes and she was having a hard time staying calm.

"Do you know why I pushed you away, Chad?" she asked, and she motioned him to sit. "Because I'm terrified! I've been alone for so long that it feels safer to build a wall around myself than to let you in. But every time you looked at me those first few months, that wall started to crack. Even if I'm scared to say it, I don't want fear to be the thing that ruins us, because I do love you. I want you... I want us. But you make me furious, and I felt like it was making me crazy and terrified!"

Chad wanted to grab her and hold her so that she would feel safe, but he knew better.

"Babe, I don't want another argument or silent days and nights. I want peace between us, love between us... you know, the kind where I can breathe again just knowing you're next to me. You feel like home, even when everything else feels like chaos. I love you too much to lose you over my mistakes that I know can be fixed, together. Please don't push me away. Let's just be together." He reached over and took her hand in his. This time, Sophie doesn't pull away, but takes his hands into both of hers.

"Chad, I don't want to fight anymore. Enough time has been wasted pushing each other away," Sophie said affectionately. "I keep pretending I can walk away, but the truth is... I don't want to. I care about you, want to hold onto you. So, I guess you win, Chad. Not because you argued harder, or because you're bigger than me," she said playfully as they both laughed. "You win because my heart won't stop reaching for you, even when my gut tells me to run. This is the kind of love people spend their lives searching for... but I do want you to know that just because you're bigger than me doesn't mean I can't kick your ass!"

"So, no more games. No more lies and especially no more 'soon to be' ex-wife because you are all mine and I don't like to share." Sophie said sternly.

Chad stood up and pulled Sophie to him. He smiled happily and said, "Oh, my love, I promise no more of any of it... I promise to only love YOU, and I'll never stop loving you. You've got my heart... hell, you had it from the first time I laid eyes on you. That's love, my beautiful woman, and I'm all in if you are."

Chapter 13

The evening brought them back to the bungalow, their love nest. When Sophie arrived, she sat in the car and stared at the bungalow. Her mind raced back to the day of their last argument there. She remembered everything said, the anger and hurt she felt… then she remembered that she was angry enough to back her car into him! She shuddered and looked around.

"This is what those damn hauntings of my past wanted me to do!" she said out loud.

Sophie wiped her eyes and thought of the happiness she felt today, and hoped that the love between them would keep her scared thoughts at bay. She grabbed her bag, the food, the wine and some candles she had bought weeks ago for the bungalow. When she reached the door, Chad opened it for her. They smiled at each other, like lovesick teenagers, and he kissed her and carried her bags for her

It seemed the storm had passed, the storm that had caused the friction between them. Storms sometimes return though, and it can be with a vengeance.

Sophie's thoughts stayed in the present when Chad handed her a glass of wine and put his arm around her waist.

He pulled her closer, gave her a passionate kiss and said, "You know what I realized while we were apart? My life doesn't mean a damn thing if it's not bound to yours."

Sophie smiled and responded, "Even though my anger and yelling, because of your lies, almost ended everything between us?"

"Especially after that," Chad said and he kissed her cheek several times. "Because it showed me, I'd rather fight with you than live in peace without you."

Sophie leaned closer. She softly said, "Then let's never let go... no more fighting. No more halfway love or anything, baby. Only everything."

"Only everything, *forever*," Chad whispered back and he kissed her deeply.

He scooped her up and carried her to the bed, moving his hands down her arms and over her sensual buttocks. She fell back on the bed as her hair fanned across the pillow, her body arching toward him. Moonlight spilled across her bare skin as he stripped away what separated them.

"Oh my... look at you, my hot, sexy woman," Chad said in his deep sounding voice.

"I'm yours," she whispered, as his lips closed around her breast, his tongue circling her nipple, drawing a cry from her. Her hands grabbed his head, urging him on as her body arched with every flick of his tongue. She ached for him to be inside of her as his kiss began to move lower and lower down her body. She was moaning and trembling as she felt his tongue inside of her hot, wet lovespot. He pleasured her until she was crying out, her body moving in rhythm with his tongue as she climaxed and collapsed onto the bed.

Sophie was almost breathless when Chad rubbed his hard penis up against her, and then her eyes opened wide. Then he entered her, their bodies joining in a rush of heat and need. She clutched at him, nails raking down his back as he moved with her, each thrust making her gasp louder. The rhythm built, urgent, relentless, tender and fierce all at once.

Their kisses were deep, their hands exploring each other's hot, sweaty bodies as their voices moaned and gasped in rhythm. He drove his hard throbbing penis into her deeper and harder until she was screaming out his name with ecstasy. And then he followed, trembling as he collapsed into her with a groan that shook through his chest, they lay tangled together, the heat of love and sweat binding them together.

Sophie's lips brushed his ear, her voice weak as she whispered, "I love you, my sweet man."

He kissed her, rough and tender all at once.

"I love you more than life, Sophie Monroe," Chad said with a growl. Wrapped in the dark. in the fire of their passion, they finally surrendered to sleep as they listened to the sounds of the water outside the bungalow and the singing of the crickets and frogs.

* * *

As the light peeked in through the window, Chad slowly opened his eyes and realized that it was morning. They were still laying in the same position they fell asleep in, wrapped in each other's arms. Chad lay there and watched Sophie sleep. He thought about last night and how deep his love had grown for her. He slowly pulled his arms away from her and touched her face and traced it to her lips. She slowly licked her lips, then moved her head as she began to awaken.

She smiled as she locked eyes with her lover. "Are you watching me sleep Mr. Thornton?" she asked in a quiet voice.

Chad gave a laugh and he said, "I can't take my eyes off your beautiful, serene face Ms. Monroe."

"I love you like I've never loved anyone," he continued in a deep, husky voice. "I don't just want your love Sophie, I want your soul bound to mine!"

She responded, trembling a little. "It already is… even when I wanted to run the other way, I know I'm still all yours."

"Say it again," Chad said, rather demanding. "Say that you're mine!"

"I'm yours, every breath, every smile, every scar, every sin," she responded, breathless.

He looked at her with piercing eyes as he said, "You know what I see? That you belong to me, Sophie, even when your anger made you want to walk away."

Her lips trembled for a long moment, then she whispered, "And if I do belong to you Chad, what happens when the fire burns everything down?"

He didn't hesitate as his hand cupped her cheek, tilting her face toward his. "Then we walk into the fire together. I'll love harder than the darkness and flames, it will never take you away from me my love."

Her eyes shimmered with both defiance and surrender, as she leaned into him, their naked bodies touching.

"You. Are. Mine." he growled against her lips.

The words undid her, she clutched his firm buttocks as the salty taste of his lips claimed hers. The kiss was not gentle. It was more like possession, a collision of anger, relief and hunger that seared straight into her soul. He kissed her deeper, as if trying to consume her completely… until their bodies found that rhythm of passion.

It was wild, reckless and consuming as his lips left hers and trailed down her throat and locked on her breast. Sophie's body arched into his with a groan and as the morning came, so did she. Wrapped in heat and rough passion, she surrendered fully… not just her body, but her soul. The fire, devotion, and love was as dangerous as the ocean beyond their window of the bungalow.

However, he was spending time at home too.

He still hadn't moved out. He hadn't been to see the lawyer about the divorce, both of which he told Sophie he had done.

Chad sometimes felt like he had a dark side. A part of him that he didn't let others see. He wasn't sure why. Could've been the PTSD. After all, intelligent people can be conniving, can even become sociopathic.

He was a smooth charmer and a lady magnet, but he always played the rather quiet, gentle soul in public.

Chapter 14

It was midweek and Chad was driving home from work. He was thinking about Sophie and her sexy body when his thoughts were interrupted by a text on his phone.

It was Rosa letting him know that both of the boys would be going to the movies with friends. Her next text said that she expected him home for dinner because she had already cooked. Chad rolled his eyes after he read that. He laughed aloud.

She really thinks she's going to demand something of me? he thought, shaking his head. *She'll see exactly who the demanding person is tonight.*

At the dining room table, Rosa poured herself some wine, and put the bottle in front of Chad. He looked up at her rather strangely, poured himself a glass.

Rosa looked hatefully back at him. "Why, you're welcome my dear husband. I'm glad you liked the dinner!"

He smirked. "Oh, thanks. It was ok."

Rosa took a deep breath. Her blood pressure was going up. She forced herself to calm down and said slowly, "I don't want to lose my temper. *I don't want to end up like sweet little Laura.*"

Chad's eyes narrowed and he got up to get something stronger to drink. "We swore we would never talk about that night again."

Rosa smirked. "And yet, it still keeps you awake, doesn't it?"

They drink in silence, remembering the body, the cover-up, the lies that sealed their union – the first time anyway. Their marriage wasn't built on love, it was built on shared guilt that couldn't be broken.

Rosa was laying in bed, staring at the ceiling when Chad joined her and smelling of bourbon. Rosa gave a little cough and she waved the smell away with her hand.

"Another drink with your ghosts?" she asked hatefully.

"Better my ghosts than your demons," he snapped back. She turned her head away sharply. Both knew what he meant.

Her affair years ago with a man who mysteriously disappeared. They don't speak of that either... the second cover-up and the sins that tied them together, but these secrets have always lingered between them.

Chad moved towards Rosa in the bed and started fondling her. She pushed his hands away and sternly said, "Are you kidding? Not tonight!"

He immediately grabbed her and straddled on top of her. She looked surprised, even a bit frightened.

He very harshly said, "Oh no, you can't refuse me. This is your 'wifely duty'. This is one of *those rules* and you will obey it! Remember the agreement you signed after I came back from the military? You *must* do what I say about satisfying me," he demanded and he glared at her.

"Don't ever forget that I have all the sex pictures of you and all those men while I was on the Navy ships. I hold the cards, Rosa and it's time for you to make your payment!"

He shoved her legs apart with his and covered her mouth. He shoved his hard throbbing penis inside her. She tried to scream but he ripped her night shirt off and shoved it into her mouth . He thrust himself hard and rough inside her. He did this for at least fifteen minutes until he finally climaxed. After, he climbed off her. She pulled the cloth out of her mouth and caught her breath.

Chad turned toward her as he said, "Remember your place. You do belong to me after all. Act the way I expect you to, or I'll take more from you next time!"

He grabbed his penis and then he smiled and said, "Oh yeah. Thanks, it was better than dinner was."

Rosa ran to the bathroom and slammed the door.

Chapter 15

The next day, Chad left work a few hours early. There was a celebration at NAS-JAX base, in honor of the squadron he had been in service with. It was the type of event that he and Rosa had attended before, always playing the perfect, happy couple. He stopped at his favorite pub before he went home. After a couple of drinks, he drove to his house and told Rosa to be ready to leave soon for the party.

They arrived at the Navy reunion with fake smiles, arm in arm. They were good at playing this game, the both of them conniving murderers. Toward the end of the evening, they ended up back in the entry way at the same time. Their masks and fake smiles dropped.

Rosa said, "They still worship you, don't they? If only they knew what you really are."

Chad turned to her.

"Careful, Rosa. If they knew about you, what you've done and saw the pictures, you'd be the one strung up or in chains anyway."

Silence followed and some of Chad's military colleagues walked into the entryway. Their fake smiles and persona switched back on. Their public perfection is their greatest lie.

The ride home was quiet, as they barely spoke to each other. Chad pictured Sophie's naked body in his head and what he wanted to do to her. Rosa drove, since Chad had a lot to drink.

She said softly, "Sometimes I wonder why we stay together."

"Because no one would put up with your antics of sexual whoring, as I have," he replied sarcastically. "And there's the complications of missing persons, so to speak."

Their marriage was a prison they both built, brick by brick, out of lies, affairs and blood. Neither could walk away without being destroyed. So, they stay, bound by hatred and secrets. They torture each other as much as possible – at least as much as Chad was willing to tolerate from Rosa.

As they walked into the house, Chad said rather happily, "I have to leave tomorrow from work, and drive to Georgia for a conference. I won't be back until Sunday evening." She nodded her head at him, but inside she was fuming. "And I'm sleeping in the other bedroom, so I don't have to listen to you move around. I need my sleep tonight."

Rosa closed the bedroom door, grabbed a pillow and screamed into it. "He infuriates me," she said to herself.

She thought he would be spending time with their sons this weekend, and that she could sneak out and meet up with her latest freak. Now she would have to deal with the boys. Maybe she could drop them off with their friends, or maybe her relatives as a backup plan?

* * *

Chad phoned Sophie the next morning on his way to work.

"Hello my beautiful woman, how are you this morning?"

"Hi baby, I'm so happy to hear your voice this morning," she said gleefully. "I'm doing great. What's up?"

"Let's meet up at the bungalow as planned. I'm going to make reservations at a quaint restaurant on the St John's River." he told her. "Sound good?"

Sophie, very excited, replied, "Yes, sounds like a plan, except... I might decide I need some dessert before dinner, if you get my drift, gorgeous man?"

"Oh babe... I can make that reservation for later. I like the way you think and I *definitely* want to attend to my woman's every need, cause I know you reciprocate very good," Chad said in that deep voice. "Have a good day sexy lady.... see you soon... I love you, babe!"

Sophie said in her sexiest voice, "I can't wait, I love you very much. Laters baby!"

Chapter 16

Saturday morning, Rosa drove the boys to the mall so they could meet up with their friends. She decided to go in and do a little shopping. She spent money like they had a never-ending pot of gold. After all, she was conniving, deceptive and very greedy. She had been in control of the purse strings for their entire marriage, so of course she had opened her own account and funneled money from the joint account where Chad's checks from the military, and now his government engineering contract job, were deposited.

But she was concerned about how she was going to keep doing that, since Chad had recently told her he was going to start taking charge of their finances.

"He's turned into such a PUTO," she said to herself in her Latin tone. "Most of the time a real IDIOTA and a PINCHE CABRÓN most recently."

As she was leaving the mall, she ran into one of Chad's work colleagues.

"Hello, Rosa. Doing some shopping?" Randy said.

"Oh, hi Randy," Rosa said, rather surprised. "Yes, I dropped the boys off here and decided I needed a little retail therapy."

Randy smiled as he asked, "Chad's not with you?"

Rosa looked at him, rather confused, and said, "No... actually, I was going to ask you why you weren't at the conference in Georgia with Chad."

Randy looked at her, confused. "What conference are you talking about? We don't have a conference going on... I'm not sure what you're talking about," he said.

Rosa took a breath as she forced a smile and said, "I must be confused as to what Chad said... well, I have to be somewhere. Nice to see you. Goodbye."

She turned and walked fast to her car, not even waiting for a response from him.

* * *

Rosa stood in her kitchen, fuming over the fact that Chad had lied about the weekend.

Her lips curled into a slow, devious smile as she thought, "So where are you hiding... and who are you hiding with?"

She started to go through his things in the dresser, then the wastebasket in his bathroom.

Suddenly, she looked at his dirty clothes basket.

She sorted through his laundry, and a crumpled slip of paper tumbled out of Chad's jeans pocket.

It was a receipt dated a few weeks ago from a gas station not far from his work.

Rosa narrowed her eyes as fury rose up in her. She knew exactly where that station was. There were beachside rentals, little getaway bungalows, on that road.

She grabbed a stack of mail. Rushing through it, she finally found the credit card statement showing rental payments for a bungalow on the same road as the gas station.

She grabbed her keys and headed straight for the bungalow.

"Let's see who you're really with!" Rosa said very angrily.

She rolled to a stop near the bungalow. Her heart pounded when she saw his Jeep in the driveway, along with a red Mercedes.

"You son of a bitch... I'm gonna kill you!" she said loudly.

The curtains were open as she caught a glimpse of Chad, shirtless. Then she saw a blonde woman walk up to him and put her arms around him as they kissed passionately.

Rosa's nails dug into her steering wheel as she watched, her suspicion hardening into rage.

"So, this is your conference," she thought. "Well, let's see how long your little love fest lasts once I'm inside."

As she started to get out, she stopped herself and thought, "No, this is not the way to handle this."

She decided to arm herself with ammunition, and when he comes home tomorrow evening, she would have him by the cajónes. She had a scheme that not only would make her the one with more to hold over Chad, but would also be very financially rewarding.

She wouldn't shout when he returned, at least not at first.

She would show him the evidence, let him sweat, and then strike, her fury timed with surgical precision to make him realize just how trapped he was.

Rosa envisioned it all in her head. She would have wine chilling, his favorite dinner on the stove, and the cool patience of a wife who knew her cheating husband had nowhere to run once she confronted him with all the evidence.

She smiled her evil smile as she carefully wove her net, thinking about every step leading up to the grand finale.

By the time Chad stepped through the door Sunday evening, Rosa planned to lure him into comfort before springing her rehearsed speech. His guard would be down, and she wouldn't give him time to lie or retreat.

She would make him pay for this. She would make them both pay for trying to make a fool out of her.

Chapter 17

When Chad arrived home Sunday evening, he was very surprised to see Rosa with her fake smile as she took his bag and handed him a glass of wine. She told him to sit down and relax as carried his bag to the bedroom.. She opened it and immediately smelled perfume on his clothes. She felt the rage rise as she pictured the blonde woman kissing her husband.

She pulled herself back together and walked into the living room, her eyes glued to Chad.

"Well, I have to say, I didn't expect to be greeted like this... hmmm, is that garlic and steak I smell?" Chad asked with a smile.

Rosa leaned down and kissed his cheek as she said, "It's your favorite meal. Thick ribeye steak, seared perfectly rare with garlic butter, roasted potatoes, and grilled asparagus. Along with your favorite wine."

Chad saw steak as his kind of meal... masculine, hearty, straightforward. He thought she was catering to his pride, but Rosa was not doting. She was catering to his arrogance in order to get him relaxed before she dropped the bomb, the truth about what she knew concerning his weekend. That way, the sweetness of her gesture made the venom of her attack even more calculated, enjoyable, and deadly.

She could not wait to plunge that knife into him, figuratively of course, and twist it until he begged.

"I will say, this meal is very good. You do know how to act the way I expect. Glad you learned your lesson," he said arrogantly.

Rosa kept her cool because she knew he would be the one learning his lesson very soon.

As he finished, she handed him a glass of bourbon and led him to the living room.

"Sit down, relax. I'll be right back," she said. "I have a surprise for you."

She walked into the bedroom and pulled a box out of her closet. Inside was evidence she had kept from when they had covered up the disappearance of *sweet little Laura*. She took the girl's bracelet and a ring off her body and hid them, exactly for the reason she needed tonight.

She also pulled out some pictures. Rosa had taken photos and a video on her phone of Chad and the blonde woman when she was spying on them at the bungalow.

She put them back in the box and walked into the living room.

Chad looked at her, his brows furrowing, and said, "What's this? I thought the surprise would be a new negligee or maybe some sex toys. I have to say, I'm a little disappointed."

Rosa had a serious look on her face as she said, "I thought you would be very tired after your long drive back from your conference in Georgia. Did you accomplish your goals while you were there? Did you get much work done without your laptop? I saw you had left it and your briefcase in the bedroom."

Chad sat up as his demeanor changed. He was taken off guard and immediately fumbled his words as he tried to think of an excuse.

Rosa laid the box on the coffee table as she boldly said, "Don't bother. I know you weren't at a conference, you liar. You think I don't know?"

She took the lid off and pulled out the pictures of him and the blonde woman. Some were rather risqué, and Chad's eyes widened as he saw pictures of him and Sophie. He did not know whether to be angry or a little scared... scared of what Rosa had done or what she might do. He knew what she was capable of and how hot-tempered his wife could be.

Then she pulled the bracelet and ring out of her pocket and said, "Recognize these?"

Chad stood up, very angry now, and yelled, "What the hell are you doing with those, you psycho bitch?"

Rosa laughed very loudly as she said, "This was always my evidence against you for when it would be needed. Guess what? Now is the time."

Chad was pacing the floor, looking at the pictures on the coffee table of him and Sophie. He was livid with Rosa and glared up at her with his demonic eyes. He grabbed her arm very tightly as his jaw tightened.

"You're pushing me too far. Where did you get these pictures of me and Sophie?"

She jerked her arm away from him with an angry look. "Don't you ever touch me again," she replied through clenched teeth.

"You think I wouldn't find out about your little secret hideaway and Sophie? You were always so weak when it came to women like her, blonde, lonely, easy to manipulate. You know, desperate."

Chad gritted his teeth and snapped back, "And you? You've had your own little cheating, carnal entanglements. Don't play like you're a saint, you two-timing whore."

They circled each other like predators as the hatred built between them.

She slammed her hand on the table. "Enough of this. You're obviously slipping, Chad. You slipped with Sophie at the bungalow and let your feelings show."

Chad took a step toward Rosa and said with icy calmness, "You need to back off and stay away from Sophie or I'll..."

"You'll what? Kill me?" Rosa stated coldly. "I don't think so, my dear. I hold all the cards, remember? Or at least the pictures and souvenirs."

Chad took a deep breath, he felt like a wall had fallen on him. He filled his glass full of more bourbon and tried to gather his composure to deal with this blow that had been thrown at him.

He and Rosa both calmed down a bit and he sat down at the table. Chad looked at her and asked rather calmly, "Ok... so what is all this really about? You think you're going to control my life now?"

Rosa shook her head and smirked. "I could control you, tell your secrets... you know, basically ruin your life! But that really doesn't interest me... for now anyway."

She poured herself another glass of wine, smiling as she said, "If you want to prove you're going to be loyal to me... then you're going to play a game with me. You can't walk away from me now without being destroyed - so you will stay and do what I say, no matter how much hatred is between us."

"You know the only games I like are sex games, of course," he said in a rough voice. "I have a feeling you're not talking about that kind of game though. What in the hell is going on in that psychotic, devious mind of yours?"

Rosa folded her arms, her eyes narrowing.

"Shut up for a few minutes, you ass. There won't be any sex games, no sex at all, unless I'm in the mood to control you. You do realize that what you did to me the other night was rape? It doesn't matter that we're married. I don't do 'wifely duties.' You should know me better than that after all these years."

She sat down beside him and, in a whispered voice, said, "It doesn't matter anymore, because I am pulling all the strings now. You will do what I say and play the game I am going to put in motion."

The cool tone in Rosa's voice sent chills down Chad's back. He knew that when she got angry or upset, it was best to move out of the way, because she would not let anything keep her from getting what she wanted.

As he sipped his bourbon, Rosa started laying out her game plan in explicit detail.

Chad leaned forward and objected, "Rosa, you're crazy if you think she's going to fall for this. She won't do it."

Rosa sneered as she said, "Crazy? No, Chad. It's calculated. Get her to agree for both of you to take out million-dollar life insurance policies. Make her believe that she's protecting you and that you're protecting her, protecting your future together. Then we will decide when her future ends."

"She trusts you, I'm guessing, and that's her weakness, Chad."

"Yours is underestimating her. Sophie's smarter than you give her credit for," he snapped back.

They shared a look, the kind that had preceded ruin for others. To Rosa, Sophie was not a person she cared about one way or another. To her, she was prey, a way to achieve the financial riches she had always thought she deserved.

Chad cared very deeply for Sophie. He truly thought he loved her, even though someone like Chad was not capable of real love, only manipulation.

"You're really talking about killing her?" he growled. "That's murder, Rosa."

She smirked and said, "Don't dress it up. You've been screwing her for months at your bungalow, by the looks of the credit card statement. That's betrayal. So I don't want to punish her. She will have to die, and we profit. Can you imagine that much money? Freedom, I tell you. Finally."

"And if I say no? I don't think I can do this because I truly care about her," he said sadly. "She doesn't deserve this. She's not like the other women I've been with."

Rosa smiled dangerously as she said, "No. She's worse, because she makes you weak. Obviously, you gave her your cajónes to hold on to. Feelings don't matter. My solutions are not hypothetical. We are both capable of ending a life when it comes to protecting ourselves," she reminded him.

"And as far as saying no to me, then you'll wish I was the one you needed to worry about instead of Sophie."

The insinuation was clear. If Chad's weakness for Sophie threatened the plan, Rosa would see to her elimination, with or without Chad's consent. Rosa knew he was a predator in disguise, just like her. The charm was in the mask, but their true power was manipulation, cover-ups, and the ruthlessness to silence anyone who threatened their secrets.

Chad felt cornered by Rosa. This had never happened before, and he was speechless for the first time since they had been married. She had broken him down and reduced him to the puppet she wanted.

Very quietly he said, "Fine... I guess I'm in since I don't really have a choice."

Rosa smiled devilishly and said to him, "No you really don't! She trusts you. She's actually blinded by it. You just have to plant the idea in her head by saying to her 'What if something happens to me, Sophie? What would you do?' She'll be begging to take out the policies for your sake and hers... for Love!"

Chad quietly asked, "And when it's done?"

Rosa replied in a cold flat tone, "Then she'll have served her purpose. We'll make sure her tragic little accident makes sense to everyone... except for her of course."

"Poor Sophie… she doesn't see the wolf in the garden," Rosa laughed sarcastically. "But she'll sign the papers, smile at you and go on believing that you're her salvation. Meanwhile, every day she lives… she's actually digging her own grave, and you get to watch her knowing that I could destroy you too, but I won't!"

Chad's head was pounding at this point from the talk of killing Sophie. Too much bourbon added to the headache as well.

"You talk like this is going to be easy," he said.

"Oh, it is. You're too weak to actually end her, Chad. That's why you need me to take control. Together we make it happen. She becomes the insurance policy, and we cash out," Rosa said with excitement.

"Do you know what I love about this plan? Well, besides the fact that I have complete control over you now," she bragged. "I'm sure Sophie still believes in love stories. What a pathetic weakness. She'll cling to you like a fool while she's dreaming of a happy ending. We'll be writing her obituary, and I think you should write it."

Chad said rather angrily, "Don't say it like that, Rosa. I care very much about her."

Rosa leaned in close and whispered, "Why not? This isn't about feelings or romance. This is business. Her signature on the policies, and Sophie becomes worth more to us dead than alive."

Chad paced the floor, trying to figure a way out of this. He couldn't understand how all of this was falling apart in front of his eyes, and it seemed there was nothing he could do to fix it.

"I never wanted it to come to this," he said as his voice cracked.

Rosa smiled. "But it has. Sophie will never see this coming. She's too deep in love. And you know what that means, don't you? Perfect for the picking," she laughed out loud.

"And the life insurance policies? How do I get them?" Chad asked.

Rosa smiled like a viper as she said, "I have a friend you will go see to get them started, and very soon they will be in Sophie's hands and signed. Her death warrant dressed up as love."

The conniving deception hung between them. They both knew they had destroyed lives before. Doing it again wouldn't be new. It would just be another sin to add to the many on their list.

Chapter 18

By mid-week, Sophie was wondering why she had not heard from Chad. Her office had been full of patients so far that week. Maybe Chad's week had been busy as well, she thought.

She sat at her desk at lunch and decided to call him. It went straight to voicemail.

"Maybe he's in a meeting. I'll send him a quick text," she thought to herself.

She started reminiscing about last weekend at the bungalow, smiling as she began to let herself truly think about a future with him. It seemed everything had gotten back on track with their love and romance.

That made her think about Rosa and the divorce. She didn't want to pressure Chad, but he hadn't said anything about the progress of the divorce since he told her he had moved out of the house and was getting things set to file. Of course, Chad had lied about that, but he had Sophie convinced everything was going well.

That evening, as she was starting to leave her office, her phone rang.

She smiled very excitedly as she said, "Well, hello stranger. I wondered if you were still alive."

Chad laughed deeply. "Hello, my beautiful woman. Who are you calling strange?"

Sophie gave out a big laugh. "I haven't heard from you this week, so I was wondering if you had left the planet."

"If I had left, you would be with me exploring the stars and making love in the Milky Way," he said in a sexy voice. "Are you heading home, babe?"

"Just walking to my car to go home. How about you, sweet man?" she purred into the phone.

"Yes, I'm heading home. I mean, to my friend's house where I'm staying," he said, fumbling for words. He felt a little panic as he almost said the wrong thing, hoping she hadn't caught on to his lie.

"Are we going to meet at the bungalow this weekend?" she asked.

"That's another reason I was calling, to see if you wanted to have a weekend of wild, erotic lovemaking in our love nest," he said in a rather cool voice.

"Of course," she said with glee. "I can't wait to see you and make sweet, hot, passionate love with you, my sex machine."

* * *

As Chad walked in the door of his house, Rosa was standing there with her arms folded and a cold glare in her eyes.

"Why haven't you picked up the forms for Sophie to sign? My friend said you have not been there, nor are you answering his calls," she yelled.

"I've been busy the last few days. I do have a job, Rosa," he blurted out.

Rosa got up in his face as she said demandingly, "I don't give a rat's ass about your job. Right now your job is to get those papers tomorrow, give them to your PRECIOUS Sophie, and convince her to sign them so we can get them approved."

Rosa was a bitch-slap-first, think-later type of person usually, but this time she had thought first in order to put this devious plan in place.

"I want that bitch in the rear-view mirror, Chad," Rosa said firmly. "You know, I really hate the anger that your sin has caused me. But then I looked at the bright side. Her demise will give me the riches I deserve, so cut her out, literally. Because what I want is all that matters, and I WILL GET IT," she said with vengeance in her voice.

Chapter 19

By Friday, Chad had the papers. He had come up with a plan of how and when he would present this idea to get Sophie on board to sign the papers. He hated doing this, deceiving her like this, but was saddened even more thinking about killing her. His feelings for her were real, well, as far as he knew what love was.

He got to the bungalow before Sophie, so it gave him time to get things set up for their romantic weekend.

He chilled her favorite wine, had scrumptious fruits, chocolates, cheeses, and other charcuterie items, even some whipped cream.

He lit the candles and laid blankets and pillows on the floor next to the view of the water and moon out the balcony doors. He wanted to have the most romantic setting for their weekend first, so he hid the papers and decided to wait until Sunday to show them to her.

When Sophie walked in, her eyes widened as big as her smile as she looked around at the romantic ambiance in the room. Chad walked out of the bedroom, wearing only a short silk kimono-style robe. His gorgeous blue eyes shimmered with the candlelight as he put his arms around her, pulling her close enough to feel his hard penis against her.

"Oh baby, it definitely feels like you're happy to see me," Sophie said as she took a few deep breaths.

"I missed you so very much… so did 'he'," he said, looking down towards his crotch area. "Did you miss 'us' too?" he asked with a devilish grin.

She reached up, cupping her hands on his face. She kissed him passionately. She found his tongue, sucking it in and out of her mouth several times. "Does that tell you how much I missed you?"

Chad got so excited, he could feel his penis growing and throbbing.

Oh my! Babe, you totally blow me away with the affection and erotic things you do to me. You have made me rock hard, see?" he said as he moved her hand inside his robe to grab his hard penis.

She felt her legs get wobbly as the passion stirred in her. He picked her up and slowly laid her on the blankets as her head rested on a pillow. He stood over her, dropped his robe, exposing himself. He knelt to undress her. She stroked his throbbing penis until she felt the heat from it, and they instantly intertwined their bodies until they became one.

Chapter 20

The next morning, Chad woke early and started making breakfast as he watched Sophie, still asleep on the blankets and pillows stacked on the floor. He looked at her, and suddenly the sadness hit him as he thought about everything that was going to happen after tomorrow. He didn't notice Sophie had sat up and was looking at him with a concerned face.

"Are you on that planet of stars again, my love?"

Chad snapped out of his daydream and realized she was staring at him. He walked over, leaned down, and kissed her cheek, lips, and then her hands. "I'm always in the stars when I'm with you, my beauty," he said rather quietly.

"Something smells good... are you cooking breakfast?" Sophie asked. "I wanted to cook for you since you made everything last time so wonderful and special."

Chad stood up as he helped her off the floor. "No, babe, I want to take care of you this weekend. I want everything to be perfect for you. You're a special part of my life. I want to show you how much you mean to me," he said lovingly.

"Then I won't argue with that. I think I like being spoiled and taken care of... especially if it's my big, handsome, intelligent man," she said as she kissed his lips.

He reached over and picked up a piece of clothing. "Here, my sexy woman, I got you a matching kimono robe so we could be twins." She squealed with joy as he draped it over her.

As they finished breakfast, they talked about many things: places they wanted to travel, sites they wanted to see, and memories they wanted to make. They even talked about wanting the same things for the future, the possibility of living together as soon as Chad's divorce was finalized. Sophie decided she would wait until tomorrow, Sunday, to ask him about the divorce situation, not knowing that Chad had his own agenda the next day too.

"I have a great idea," Chad said with a big smile. "It's a beautiful sunny day, we could go to that beach that's not far from here."

Sophie put her arms around his neck. "I think that's a great idea. I'm definitely in need of some Vitamin D. I've seen a cool looking bar and grill place right on that beach. They provide lounge chairs, umbrellas, and a small table to hang out on the beach, as long as you buy food and drink there."

"I think we have a plan, you sexy woman," he said as he kissed her passionately. "Or we could stay here and have a crazy day of wild naughty sex!"

Sophie giggled as she felt him push his penis up against her. "As tempting as that is, I think we need to get out and enjoy some sunshine, beach, and water time." She grabbed his firm buttocks as she whispered, "Then we can come back later and have a steamy hot shower together. How's that sound, baby?"

"This is one of the reasons I love you, my sexy blonde. You have the best ideas that always make me want to be with you, be inside of you, and just stay there forever," he whispered back as he kissed her neck.

She felt her body quivering and responding to his touch. She took his head in her hands and said, "My love, you excite me every time you touch or kiss me. But right now, we need to not do this, or we will never stop."

Chad dropped his head like a disappointed little child but looked back up and gave a demonic laugh. "Ok, you're right, but when we get back, we're going to enjoy that hot steamy shower until it turns cold!"

Sophie smiled as she turned to go to the bedroom. Chad slapped her soft, tight buns. She jumped and giggled as he said in that deep voice, "You're mine, Sophie Monroe. Don't forget that!"

They enjoyed their day at the beach as they played in the ocean and walked up the beach gathering seashells. They also lounged in their chairs, staring at the water as the sun made it sparkle like diamonds. The beach server from the bar and grill brought them food and drinks. It was a perfect day.

They drove back to the bungalow, enjoyed their steamy shower for several hours, and ended their day watching the sun disappear as they sat by the water on their deck. They finished a bottle of wine and some shots of tequila before going to bed.

Even though they had a full day of sun and beach, lots of sex and alcohol, Chad didn't sleep much. He tossed and turned and his mind raced, thinking about what he was going to do to convince Sophie to sign the papers. He had many scenarios in his head, but he was also feeling pain and guilt at what would happen down the road. He had never had feelings like these before.

He quietly got out of bed when the sunrise peeked out over the water. He didn't want to disturb Sophie right now. He walked out on the deck and looked at the sunrise, hoping that this wouldn't be the last time he would be here with her. He wasn't sure she would see things his way, and wasn't sure he knew how to convince her. But he also knew that if he didn't succeed, Rosa would destroy his life, and he would never see Sophie again. What was he thinking?? He was never going to see her again either way...

He didn't know whether to scream or cry.

Chad pulled himself together and walked back in to make coffee and breakfast. Sophie still slept. He had Mimosas chilling in the fridge. He was making a special breakfast with all of her favorites. When he finished setting the table, Sophie walked out of the bedroom.,

She smiled and said, "Mr. Thornton you're spoiling me... and I think I could get used to it!" He grabbed her, kissed her and hugged her so tight.

He never wanted to let her go. Sophie hugged him too, but wondered what was going on.

They finished their breakfast, and both were full and satisfied. Chad told her that he would clean up the dishes in a little while. They took their Mimosas out to the deck and cuddled together on the big porch swing. He just wanted to enjoy the morning before he had to convince her to sign the life insurance papers. Sophie was touching and rubbing his chest. She expressed her love and gratitude about the weekend of paradise he had created for her.

He kissed her lips and said, "I would do anything for you, Sophie... you are the best thing in my life right now. I just want to hold you forever."

Sophie started to head back inside and took Chad by the hand. "I'm going in to get some more Mimosas... come with me sweet man, because I hear the bedroom calling us!"

Chad poured more champagne into their glasses, as much as he wanted to be inside of her and pleasure her, he was afraid she would think he was manipulating her with sex when he asked her to sign the papers.

"Here you go babe. Actually, can we sit down here? I have something important that I need to talk to you about," he said seriously.

Sophie grew serious, too. "Ok honey, I'm listening."

He went to the bedroom and walked out with a file folder in his hand. Sophie appeared confused, but also very curious to see what was in it.

As he sat down at the table beside Sophie, he laid the folder on it and started talking.

"Remember how we were talking about building something real for us? A home, a future? I'm serious about being in this for the long haul, babe." He laid his hands on hers and her heart squeezed at his words. He sounded so steady, so protective. Yet she couldn't help but wonder what this was really about.

"What's this mystery about Chad? What's in the file folder?"

"Sophie, listen, with the kind of job you have, working with patients that could be sick or contagious and me working directly with the government, mostly military issues, we're not invincible." He took a deep breath and pulled the papers from the folder. "I want to love and protect you so much that I thought this was the way to do it... for both of us."

She picked up the papers and her eyes darted back and forth, reading the page. The bungalow was quiet, the only sound was a faint hum of the ceiling fan above them. Chad leaned back in his chair, studying Sophie with that practiced steadiness of sharp eyes and mouth softened into what looked almost like concern.

Sophie laid the papers down calmly, folded her arms, uneasy, and then quietly said, "These are life insurance policies... Each worth a million dollars? You're showing me these... but you're not even divorced yet! I was going to ask you about the progress of the divorce later today, but I didn't want to seem like I was pressuring you. Why did you have these drawn up now, Chad?"

His jaw tightened just for a moment and then he replied, "I'm saying life doesn't wait. One car accident, one bad call, and everything we want to build could be gone in a flash. Don't make this about suspicion, babe."

Suspicion? Sophie thought. *His eyes are too sharp, too calculating. Is this more about power than love?*

"You're still married to *her*, but you're asking *me* to sign these policies?" she asked, feeling cornered.

Chad's tone changed quickly as he answered, "That's why I wanted to spoil you this weekend with everything, so I could make you feel special and loved… you know, sort of a celebration. I've signed the final papers and Rosa's lawyer is having her sign this week. She's already agreed to everything, and then the divorce will be finalized before the life insurance policies will be in force!" Chad surprised himself with how quickly he came up with that lie.

"Maybe you should have led with the divorce news before you laid insurance papers in front of me to sign," she replied, sounding a little calmer but still hesitant. "So why does your reason for my signature sound like desperation more than love and protection?"

Chad's eyes darted around as if he were looking for a monitor to read from as he searched for words in his head. Finally, he breathed and blurted out, "That's just paranoia talking. You know I love you and want to protect you. I would never hurt you, Sophie," even as he heard himself lying to her.

Sophie's head snapped toward him, her voice getting louder. "That's exactly what someone would say before they do it!"

The fan whirred overhead, filling the silence that followed. He pressed on, his voice more urgent now. "Sophie, you see tragedies every day. Families torn apart because someone thought they had more time. Do you want that to happen to us?"

He sounded so sincere and caring, she thought, maybe because part of her wanted to believe he was just being loving and responsible. Maybe he was right, at least about one thing. Life could be cruel. Maybe she was a fool for hesitating, but deep down she felt a chill, like this policy was not just paper but a contract of her own doom.

"You make it sound like danger is waiting at the door." Her throat tightened as she continued. "No, I don't want that to happen to us either. God, I've seen enough families suffer over my years of being a nurse."

As Chad held her hands again, he said calmly, "That's life, babe. You protect what you love, and I love you. Don't you want that safety net for us too?"

Chad leaned closer, lowering his voice. "All I'm asking for is a signature. Trust in me. We each hold a policy for a million dollars. No tricks, no deceit, just protection for our future."

For a heartbeat, she saw the man who had promised forever beneath the stars. Maybe this was about trust, and even hope. She looked at him, her chest tightening. "Part of me wants to believe you, that maybe you're the Chad that loves me, the one who makes me feel safe."

"Then believe it. Let's do this together," he replied. "This is love, real love, Sophie. Steps toward commitment, protection, permanence. Don't wait. Sign with me so we can protect our future together."

She saw a flash in his eyes. She thought it looked like frustration, maybe a bit of anger that he was trying to hide. She started wondering again if this was more about control than love.

Sophie stood up, took a few steps, and finally cleared her throat. "You've said a lot of things this weekend and given me much to think about. I'm not a person to make rash decisions, especially when it comes to something this big," she said, pointing to the papers. "I need you to give me a few days to think about it. This way I can read everything in order to make an exact decision."

She picked up the papers and file folder, went to pack her stuff, and drive home. Chad was speechless as he watched her go. His fury and anger were getting the best of him as he thought, what the hell am I going to tell Rosa? I don't want to have to deal with her wrath of being the bitch that she is.

As Sophie drove away, Chad stood there, his expression in shock. "What have I done? I can't believe I let her leave with the insurance policies. Why was I not able to convince her?" he thought to himself.

He walked back into the bungalow, poured himself a drink, walked out to the deck, and began to think of a plan. He knew Rosa was going to erupt like a volcano, so he had to figure out how to keep that from happening. He stayed there the rest of the afternoon, avoiding Rosa's wrath for a while anyway. He came up with an idea to resolve the situation and hoped Rosa would go along with it in order to get Sophie's signature that week and keep Rosa from using the evidence she had against him.

Chapter 21

It's late in the evening when Chad returns home, tossing his keys down. He saw Rosa sitting at the table with a glass of wine. She stared at him and asked, "Well... is it done?"

Chad carefully walked toward her as he said, "She didn't sign yet. Sophie wanted to take the papers with her, just to look them over. Said she'll decide in a couple of days."

Rosa snapped her head up, her voice sharp as glass. "She what? You let her walk out of there with them?"

Chad shrugged as he calmly said, "She just needs a couple of days. That's normal, Rosa. It makes her feel safer. She just wants to feel like she's in control."

Rosa slammed her glass down, wine splashing onto the table. "Normal? Nothing about this is normal, Chad! And you handed her control? We don't have time for this. Do you even realize what you've done? Any idea what you've risked?" Her voice rose, followed by a bitter laugh.

Chad snapped back, "She'll sign. Don't you get it? She's hooked on me. Relax, she trusts me." Lying to Sophie and now lying to Rosa. There was the real Chad, devious, manipulative, and narcissistic.

Rosa leaned across the table, her eyes burning like fire as she spoke low but firmly. "If she starts second-guessing, if she talks to the wrong person, everything will unravel. If she shows anyone those papers, don't think for one second I won't tell your sons and the whole world your lies and secrets. Hell, I'll tell them this was all your idea. You'll be the one with blood on your hands, not me."

Chad grimaced. "She won't. I have her trust."

Rosa pressed a finger to his chest as she said in a low, lethal voice, "If she doesn't cooperate, I'll make sure your name is carved in every headline. Fraud, adultery, conspiracy. You'll drown in it, and I'll paint you guilty before she even opens her mouth."

Chad's jaw tightened, his fists clenching as he met her gaze and said, "Careful, Rosa."

Her cold smile ran through him.

"No, YOU be careful. If Sophie ruins this, I'll expose every filthy thing you've done. Navy boy, hero on paper, murderer in truth," she replied through clenched teeth. "Don't test me. Don't underestimate me, Chad. You think you're dangerous? Try crossing me when I have nothing left to lose."

Her words hung in the air, sharp as broken glass. For once, she saw anger flicker across his face before he buried it. And for the first time, Rosa realized that she might have pushed him into showing who he really was.

Chad took a few steps away from her and then took some deep breaths to calm his rage.

He had come up with a plan at the bungalow, and as he turned to face her he said, trying to stay calm, "I have a plan that will convince her to sign the papers. I told Sophie that our divorce was set, and that you would be signing them this week. That way, the divorce would be complete before the insurance policies were in force."

She looked at him and started to object, but he put his hand up to stop her from speaking.

He continued, "Now, I need you to get this friend of yours that drew up the policies to also draw up divorce papers that look legit. You sign them, and I'll show Sophie it's a done deal. I know she'll sign the policies if she sees the divorce papers. That will put her full trust in me. It shows that I do what I told her I would."

Rosa stood there quietly for a few minutes, then she spoke. "This was not in the plan, but I guess if it makes her sign, then I guess it's the way to fix the debacle you caused. Fine! I'll get him to draw up the divorce papers for us to sign. You take them to her immediately. I want this done NOW, or heads will roll, and yours will roll all the way to prison. Do you understand?" she snapped.

* * *

By midweek, Rosa had signed the fake divorce papers and given them to Chad. He immediately contacted Sophie to ask if she would meet him for lunch at the bungalow.

Sophie was in her office working when she got distracted and stared at the life insurance forms spread out on her desk. "Am I protecting us or sealing my fate, maybe even digging my own grave?" she wondered.

Her phone buzzed. She didn't need to check to know it was Chad. She hesitated, then answered. "Hi hon, what's going on?"

Chad's voice on the phone was steady as he tried to make it sound excited too. "Hey babe, I hope I'm not interrupting. I wanted to see if you would meet me for lunch at the bungalow. I have something to tell you... it's good news," he tried to sound convincing.

She wasn't sure what to say. She didn't want him pressuring her, but she finally agreed to be there.

Chapter 22

Sophie pulled in the driveway of the bungalow, she walked in and Chad was standing there with a huge smile. She saw that he had the table set with their favorite Thai food. She smiled hesitantly. "How sweet... It smells great. What's all this about, Chad?" she asked.

"I wanted us to have a bit of a celebration," he cooed and he kissed her on the forehead. "Please, sit down and let me show you something."

She sat at the table and he lay a folder in front of her. She opens it and glances at the divorce papers. She looked at him and was not sure what to say.

"She signed the divorce papers like I told you. This is a copy, the lawyer has taken the originals, and they've been submitted by the courts. It's all said and done. I'm finally free of her!" he said, lying through his teeth.

Sophie took a deep breath and happily said, "I'm so happy for you... for us! I guess I should have never doubted you."

Chad leaned down and kissed her tenderly as she touched his face. "I love you very much, babe. I would have brought Champagne, but I figured you would have to go back to work. But we can at least celebrate with this wonderful food and just be here together."

She agreed as they toasted with their forks. Chad decided he would let her eat before he talked about signing the policies.

They sat at the table looking at each other when they finished lunch. Sophie took his hand and said, "Thanks for this. The food was delicious, and the company was wonderful. The reason you asked me here is the icing on the cake. I needed to see this, baby."

Chad squeezed her hand as he replied, "I'm happy we're here together and able to get this hurdle behind us. I want us to move forward with the future we talked about. We can do everything now." He was trying to reassure her that there was nothing and no one standing in their way.

Chad stood up, put the divorce papers and folder into his briefcase, then leaned against the counter and casually said, "Now that you see the papers signed and the divorce is final, there's no reason you can't sign the policies. This can be our first step toward our future."

He kept talking as he saw her expression change. "Babe, it's just smart planning. Couples do this all the time. You trust me, don't you?"

Sophie said softly, "I... I want to. I'm just not sure what this could mean."

Chad put his arms around her waist and whispered in her ear, "It means security. It means us... forever!"

She grabbed her purse and pulled out the papers, smiling as she handed them to him.

She had signed them before she came to the bungalow, even though the moment the ink dried she felt both relief and dread wrap around her at the same time. When Chad showed her the divorce papers, the doubt began to fade, and she decided she had made the right decision to sign them.

His mouth almost dropped open, but he knew he needed to keep his calm demeanor. He took the papers, laid them on the counter, and grabbed Sophie, kissing her lips until she opened hers. Their tongues circled each other as if they were doing a happy dance.

He gazed at her with the mesmerizing look he was good at. "My love, you have made me so happy. You trust me again, and now we have taken that first step toward our future," he said.

His fake smile covered up his own thoughts of still being able to manipulate someone. "I want to carry you to the bed and kiss every part of your body, make love to you over and over until we explode into ecstasy at the same time."

Sophie giggled her naughty laugh and said, "I love that idea... but I do have to get back to work. I'm late now." She glanced at her watch. "I'm sorry that I can't stay longer, sweet man... let's celebrate this weekend. See you back here Friday?" She opened the door, turned around and said, "I love you Chad Thornton."

Chapter 23

By Friday morning, Sophie was trying to get her afternoon patients rescheduled. Chad had told her the day before that they needed to meet at the bungalow by two o'clock. He was having the insurance guy (Rosa's friend), meet them there to sign the final draft because they had to have a witness for their signatures. Sophie felt a little uneasy and unsure why they had to do this today, but she told him she would be there.

When she arrived, introductions were made as they sat down at the table.

"These are the final drafts. Everything has been approved for the policies for each of you. I just need routine signatures for them to be in force... here and here," said the insurance guy, pointing to the papers.

Sophie hesitated, her fingers trembling. Chad whispered in her ear, "Remember, you're doing this for us. For our future, my love."

His voice was low and steady, the one he used when he wanted her to bend. She bent. She pressed the pen down and signed. When it was done, she laid the pen down and breathed a sigh of relief. Chad gave her thigh a slow squeeze under the table, his grin flashing with victory.

After the guy left, Sophie and Chad stood there silently, looking at each other. He pulled her close, and their mouths found each other with urgency replacing hesitation. She clung to him, his hands tracing her curves as though her signature had bound her body to him. Her hesitation melted into heat, her pulse mixing fear and desire. She was a little afraid of what she had given him, but felt addicted to the way his dominance consumed her.

Chad grabbed her soft, sweet bum and lifted her up on the counter. They immediately tore at each other's clothes. Both their pants dropped to the floor, and Chad thrust his hard, throbbing penis inside her tight, wet sweet spot. As she screamed with ecstasy, their bodies rocked in rhythm once again.

Chapter 24

The next week unfolded deceptively calm, filled with busy workdays, quiet dinners, and late-night phone calls. Sophie was feeling happy to be with Chad again, and she thought they were working toward a real future.

However, there were always lingering thoughts of fear and wondering if something evil was coming. Those thoughts threatened to pull her back into panic from the past, so she tried to think positively, believing that Chad was being honest and that he truly loved her.

Chad had informed Rosa that he was going to move some of his clothes and belongings to the bungalow and stay there for now.

"This is the best idea in order to make it appear that the divorce is real and final," he told her.

"I agree for once. I think you should stay there. It will make little Sophie believe that you're divorced. This way, staying close to her will make it easier to plan her demise," Rosa said in a devious voice.

Chad was surprised that she agreed with his idea. He didn't have to fight with her about it.

He packed some things and drove to the bungalow. It was late, so he decided he would wait and surprise Sophie with his news when she arrived on Friday evening. He settled into the bungalow and thought about how glad he was not to be under the same roof as Rosa. Still, he missed his boys. They were very upset with him when Rosa had told them that she and Chad were divorcing.

When Sophie arrived at their love nest Friday evening, she saw all the clothes and personal items Chad had there. She looked at him confused.

"I decided since I'm divorced that I should just move here for now. Maybe we can spend even more time together," he said as he kissed her. "See nothing's changed except for my residence. Just you and me, the way it should be."

Sophie, holding him close, responded, "You make it sound so easy."

Chad cupped his hand to her cheek and said, "Because it is. Stop overthinking."

She craved the way he touched her, the way he made her feel both alive and on the edge of danger. Still her gut kept tightening with feelings that she didn't want to think about.

Their night blurred into bodies tangled in sheets that became slick with sweat. Sophie whispered and screamed Chad's name until they slipped into a satisfied slumber after their wild erotic sex games.

The next couple of days and nights were a blur at the bungalow, their private cocoon. They drank coffee on the deck at sunrise, their laughter mingling with the sound of waves. At night, they toasted wine under the moon on the deck, and the water shimmered like diamonds.

Chad kissed her hard, pulling her down into a pile of blankets. The night was thick with crickets, the air electric as his touch made her body arch. Fear threatened through her pleasure, but she let herself fall deeper, intoxicated by the danger.

* * *

Sophie woke very early while it was still dark outside. She had started having one of the scary nightmares but woke herself before it developed full-blown. She stood by the window while Chad was sleeping naked on the bed.

Her mind wandered to the insurance policies, and she thought to herself, "Have I given him everything? If I let the fear win, I might lose him. If I trust him, maybe I lose myself. But God help me, I can't let go!"

Sophie decided to cling to this fragile normal, convincing herself this was the right choice.

Chad stirred, opening his eyes, he looked over and saw Sophie staring out the window.

"What are you thinking, my sexy lover?" Chad asked quietly.

Sophie looked back at him with a half-smile and responded, "That I've never felt this close to someone and it scares me a little."

He reached for her hand, pulling her back to bed as he whispered, "Then let fear make it sweeter."

They made love slowly, deliberately, and his movements wavered between surrender and resistance. Each kiss tasted like both devotion and doom. Their bodies rocked until they climaxed... and fell back on the bed.

Chad wrapped his arms and body all around Sophie as he kissed her face, lips and head.

Chad quietly whispered, "You belong to me now, my love."

They slowly fell asleep in each other's arms.

Chapter 25

For the next few weeks, they lived in their own little world, wrapped in the safety of their love nest cocoon. In addition to their weekends together, Sophie stayed over a few nights during the week, since the drive to work from Chad's place was not far. Her life felt magical with Chad in it, or at least she believed it was magical.

But just like a magician who only lets the audience see one side of the illusion while the other hand worked unseen, Chad was hiding far more than Sophie realized.

Their mornings were filled with promise, their nights soaked in passion. Sophie told herself this was love. This was trust. This was normal. Each time she whispered those reassurances into the darkness, she almost believed them.

Meanwhile, Rosa had been plotting the details of Sophie's demise. The thought of cashing in a million dollar life insurance policy thrilled her, especially once Chad disposed of Sophie. Greed sharpened her cruelty, making her more devious and conniving by the day. She wanted everything, and she even began to wonder how she might take Chad's share of the money as well.

She texted him constantly, questioning his plans and pushing for it to be done soon. What Rosa failed to realize was that she was creating a paper trail, one Chad had already decided to use against her, ensuring that she would be the one to take the fall for Sophie's murder.

Chapter 26

Two weekends later, Sophie brought her favorite wine and Chad's bourbon to the bungalow. She really needed a weekend of chilling and seeing his gorgeous face. The week had been brutal at work. She had trained two new nurses and learned a new computer system, all while keeping up with her normal duties. She knew the weekend would be relaxing with Chad by her side, and even though the unsettling feeling in her gut was still there, she chose to ignore it.

"The heart wants what the heart wants," she told herself.

As she pulled into the driveway of the bungalow, she looked around for Chad's Jeep. It was not there.

She walked inside, glanced at her watch, and wondered where he was? He left work a little earlier than she did.

She shrugged and began chilling the wine.

Chad walked in a little while later as Sophie was pouring him a glass of bourbon. She looked up and froze at the sight of him. His hands were full, holding a bouquet of beautiful flowers and a gourmet dinner from the seafood restaurant down the road.

He wore a silly smile as he said, "Hi beautiful! I'm late and you beat me here, damn it."

She smiled widely as she took the food and handed him the glass of bourbon. She kissed him and said in a sexy voice, "I'm glad I was here, but I should have greeted you naked!"

"Oh babe! That would have been an even lovelier sight than I've had in a minute."

He handed her the flowers as he kissed her and said, "Beauty for my beauty." He then took her hand and laid it on his hard penis.

"And that's also for you, whenever you want it," he said in a low, seductive voice.

Sophie giggled as she traced him with her finger, feeling his pants tighten as he grew harder. She wrapped her hand around him as if he were a handle and guided him toward the bedroom with a devious smile. Chad pulled his shirt off as she led him into their magical room of ecstasy.

About an hour later, they emerged from the bedroom in their kimono robes, their hair tousled. They looked at one another and burst into laughter, pointing at each other like little kids. They went to the kitchen, where Chad began heating the food he had brought while Sophie poured a glass of wine for each of them.

After dinner, they walked out onto the deck and toasted their happiness. The water glowed under the bright full moon. The only sounds were crickets, frogs, and the gentle splash of water against the deck. The peacefulness made Sophie feel calm and happy, and for the first time in a while, she did not feel scared.

Chad tried to feel the same as he put on his fake smile, but inside he was fighting his demons. His thoughts drifted to his next scheme, even as he struggled against the growing urge to protect her.

Lost in his thoughts, he did not realize Sophie had stepped back inside. She lit all the candles and fluffed the blankets and pillows on the floor.

She was pouring another glass of wine when he came back in. He immediately said, "You're such a vision, babe! The candlelight dances all around you, yet you're the brightest light I see, my beautiful star!"

He kissed her, and Sophie poured him another glass.

"Thank you, sweet man. I wanted to give our love nest some ambiance to go with our sweet lovemaking."

Chad clinked glasses with her as they sat down on the blankets.

As they drank their wine and talked, Sophie confessed, "I thought I'd feel, um... trapped after we signed the papers. But right now, I just feel alive," she said with relief.

"That's because you're mine, completely!" he said as he took their glasses and set them aside.

His kiss was deliberate, his touch slower now, as though savoring her surrender. She gave herself to him, her body arching beneath his as he pressed her back against the pillows. Their bodies were urgent and desperate, Chad's breath hot against her ear as they both began to moan while he pulled his hard, throbbing penis in and out of her.

Between moans, he whispered, "Mine forever, no turning back."

Her lips trembled as she answered, panting and shaking, "No turning back."

With that, Chad pushed himself inside her very rough, overwhelming her with ecstasy as she screamed and climaxed.

* * *

The sun was shining brightly on Sunday morning when Sophie opened her eyes, realizing they had slept through the sunrise. She headed to the kitchen to start the coffee and make a wonderful breakfast. She wanted to spoil Chad the way he had spoiled her.

The sounds from the kitchen woke Chad when he realized Sophie was no longer in bed beside him. He sat up and took a deep breath, trying to clear his mind of thoughts about the plan for her murder. Putting on his best fake smile, he walked quietly into the kitchen and slipped his arms around her waist.

She startled, then relaxed into his touch. Turning, she gave him a loving smile and a kiss.

"Good morning, my gorgeous woman. What smells so good?" he asked.

Sophie poured him a cup of coffee as she replied, "It's still my time to spoil you, so I have some of your favorite things cooking."

He took a drink and said, "How did I get so lucky to have a woman like you in my life? You have no idea how much you've changed my life, and I love you so much for that."

Sophie sat down in his lap, her arms around his neck, and kissed him passionately as she whispered, "I think we're both blessed to have each other, to have found so much love in a total blessing!"

After breakfast, they drove to the sandy beach down the road. They spent the beautiful sunny day in the water and on the sand, enjoying drinks and a few appetizers. They returned to the bungalow in the early afternoon so they could spend more time alone before the day ended.

Sophie decided to shower first and invited Chad to join her, but he made an excuse, saying he needed to call his boys.

Rosa had been blowing up his phone all morning, demanding to know when he was going to start putting the plan in place to get rid of "Little Sophie."

He stepped out onto the deck, phone pressed to his ear as he called the woman he now thought of as a bitch, telling her to back off and stop bugging him. Their voices rose as they tried to talk over one another.

Chad did not realize Sophie had finished her shower and was standing by the bedroom window. Hearing raised voices, she moved closer, trying to understand what was happening.

She caught only fragments of what Chad was saying. "I said I'd handle it. You've given me no choice, have you? Stop texting me, Rosa. Don't forget, if this goes wrong, both of us are burned!"

Confused and shaken, Sophie stepped back into the bathroom. Why was he talking to Rosa? Her hand trembled as she dropped a bottle onto the floor.

Hearing the noise, Chad snapped his head toward the window, but he saw no one there. He ended the call, unease settling in his chest as he wondered if Sophie had overheard the conversation.

She dressed quickly, forcing herself to stay calm. She decided to act normal, as though nothing was wrong. When she went into the kitchen, Chad was just stepping back through the glass doors.

Without turning to face him, she asked how his call with his boys had gone.

Chad breathed a quiet sigh of relief, assuming she had not heard anything. "They're doing okay, but Logan, the younger one, is still upset with me. At least he talked to me a little," he lied.

"Well, that's good. It's your turn to shower now. I'll clean up the rest of the mess here," she said as she turned to look at him.

He agreed, set his phone down on the counter, and walked through the bedroom.

Great, now I can look at his phone, she thought.

Sophie lingered at the counter, her nerves vibrating from what she had overheard minutes earlier. Compelled by dread, she caught her breath as her thumb slid across the screen and typed in his code. Her stomach flipped as she scrolled through the texts from Rosa. Message after message glared back at her, Rosa's words sharp and venomous, like pages torn from a nightmare.

Rosa: The insurance policies are signed and in force. It's time to take care of business. Don't get soft, Chad. You have lied long enough. Follow through!

Chad: I'm working on it. She's close, but I need more time.

Rosa: No more delays. An accident at the bungalow. A drowning looks natural. No suspicion. No one will question it.

Sophie froze. Her pulse hammered in her ears, her throat tightening as the truth crystallized. Her blood ran cold.

Rosa, his ex wife, the fucking bitch.

They were not just using her. They were planning her death. And the man she had let back into her heart was at the center of it all.

The pieces fell together in sickening alignment. Sophie covered her mouth, choking back a cry. Every word confirmed it. They had been planning this for weeks.

The phone burned in her hand like evidence from hell.

She knew she had only minutes to think. Her choice was stark. Confront him now and risk that he might kill her immediately? Or play along until she could escape with her life?

She questioned her sanity. Was this really happening?

As the panic intensified, she felt herself teetering on the brink. She had uncovered a horrific plot against her. The words on the screen bound her more tightly than any signature ever could. Deep inside, she knew the ink on those papers had already tied her to a fate she might not escape.

When Chad stepped out of the bathroom, he saw Sophie gathering her things, clearly preparing to leave.

She calmly told him that her assistant had called to remind her she had forgotten an important brief at the office for her meetings out of town that week. She said she needed to stop by her office to retrieve them and then head home to work.

Chad looked confused but said he understood. Sophie kissed him quickly and practically ran out the door.

As she sped down the road, panic finally broke free. Sophie screamed as loud as she could, the sound tearing out of her chest as she drove away.

Chapter 27

Sophie stared at herself in the bathroom mirror late that night, her hands trembling as she gripped the sink.

She whispered to her reflection, "They think they can kill me, drown me like I'm disposable, like I don't see through them. I know what it feels like to keep a secret in the dark. Maybe I've gotten rid of things in my past too."

Her reflection seemed to glare back at her in judgment. Sophie shook her head, her voice cracking. "No, that was different. That was survival. I didn't have a choice."

She leaned closer to the mirror, her eyes seeming to glow as a low growl slipped from her throat. "Chad thinks I'm blind and easy to manipulate. Rosa thinks I'm weak. They really don't know me at all. I'll make them regret pulling me into their game."

Echoes stirred in her subconscious, like a faint knock, the sound of the past clawing its way forward. Sophie closed her eyes and whispered, "God forgive me. I do know what I'm doing this time."

She sat down on the bed and picked up her phone, debating whether to call the police, a friend, anyone. Instead, she dialed a number she knew by heart, someone she had not spoken to in years. Her finger hovered over the call button as doubt crept in.

Maybe I shouldn't drag them into this. Everything could come out. The accident. The blood. They'd never believe a self defense plea from back in her past. They'd probably say I'm no different from Chad and Rosa.

Her phone buzzed suddenly, Chad's name flashing across the screen.

Sophie hissed at it. "You son of a bitch snake. Smile at me, kiss me, all the while you're planning my funeral behind my back."

The buzzing stopped. Silence followed.

"I don't need the police. I don't need anyone in this mess," she said softly to herself. "I just need to be smarter than both of you. You two set the rules. Guess what? I'm going to rewrite them."

She closed her phone, her hands steady now.

Sophie sat at the kitchen table with a glass of wine, contemplating how to burn their world down. Sleep refused to come. She paced through the apartment, every creak of the floorboards sounding like a warning. Every shadow felt like someone standing over her.

She refused to let fear blind her again.

Anxiety from the past surged forward, memories clawing their way back. She remembered the screams in her head, the way she had told herself it was the only way. The past was supposed to stay buried.

But the past had teeth, and now it was biting back.

"You want a game, Chad?" she said aloud, her voice sharp. "You want me gone, Rosa? Fine. But I don't die easy. I'll bleed you both dry before I let you write my ending. No matter what it takes."

The sound of her own laughter echoed through the room, chilling her to the bone.

* * *

On Monday morning, Sophie arrived at work earlier than usual. She had been awake all night. When her assistant arrived, Sophie told her she would be working from home for the next few days on special reports for one of the doctors.

After finishing some computer work, she left a few hours later to head home, with one important stop to make first.

Sophie drove slowly up the road toward the bungalow, making sure Chad was still at work. His Jeep was not in the driveway. She glanced at the Thai restaurant nearby. He was not there either.

"Good," she murmured.

She pulled in and entered the bungalow quickly. Heading straight to the bedroom, she prayed Chad had not moved the papers. She opened the drawer where he had placed them weeks earlier.

They were still there.

Sophie exhaled in relief and removed the folder. She scanned both insurance policies and sent copies to her private email. A slow grin spread across her face.

"They think I'm afraid and that they've already won," she muttered. "Not this time. The tables will be turned, on both of them."

She straightened her body after she returned the papers to the folder. Calmer now, her plan was set.

She heard the demon voice in her head softly say, *You've always been good at this, Sophie.* She closed her eyes, imagining Chad's face turning from smug confidence to utter horror!

Now that Sophie was aware of Chad and Rosa's conspiracy, she made the decision to play along. On the outside, she would be the devoted lover, while internally she plotted revenge with careful precision.

* * *

It was Tuesday morning, and she had not answered Chad's texts or calls. Instead, she sent a voice message, knowing it would keep him satisfied and out of her way for the rest of the week while she finalized her plans for the two demons who thought they owned her fate.

Hi baby. My apologies for not being able to contact you before now. As I told you Sunday at the bungalow, I'm out of town this week with many meetings. I've been bogged down all day, even leading to work meetings at dinner. I'll be back late Friday night, so I'll see you at the bungalow on Saturday. I love you, honey.

There, she thought. That gave her the entire week to finish planning Chad and Rosa's end.

Sophie sat at her vanity, staring into the mirror as her reflection slowly blurred into something darker. The demons whispered in her mind, reminding her of what she was capable of.

You've done this before. You know how to smile while you sharpen the knife.

A slow, dark smile spread across her lips. Her eyes seemed to glow as her reflection stared back, darker now, nodding like an accomplice. Sophie knew exactly what she was going to do, and she spent the next several days putting her plan into motion.

Her inner demons drove her forward, shaping a chilling revenge.

Sophie smirked as she said aloud, "They think they can play nurse and patient with me, that I'll just lie down and die for their money. They better think again. I know the body better than anyone. I know the places where silence can be forced in an instant."

Chapter 28

That same night, Rosa summoned Chad home. He walked in, poured himself a glass of bourbon, and sat at the table. He sipped slowly while Rosa paced, furious.

"You said this would be done. Why is she still breathing?" Rosa demanded.

Chad replied calmly, "I told you earlier today that I need a little more time. We can't rush around leaving footprints, Rosa. If something happens too soon, who do you think the cops will look at first? Me? Or you, the grieving wife who is jealous of and despises the mistress?"

"Don't you dare think you're going to pin this on me, you bastard," Rosa snapped. "I'm not the one who's going to rot in a cell!"

"Relax. I'm not trying to pin anything on you," he said, lying smoothly. "I'm just saying if anyone is going to be suspected, it might be you first. The jealous wife, the motive already there. The story writes itself."

Chad kept his face calm, smiling inside at the thought of her behind bars.

"What the hell does that mean, Chad?" Rosa asked, narrowing her eyes.

He grinned, delivering the words he had rehearsed. "Police love stories that look straightforward. The jealous wife, fingerprints at the bungalow. Maybe even texts about murder. Textbook. Case closed."

Rosa walked towards him, murder flashing in her eyes.

Her voice was sharp and threatening as she said, "Don't think you're going to set me up, husband. I have no problem pulling out all the stops to make you disappear. Don't forget, I know how to play this game too."

Chad stood slowly and stepped closer, his voice cold. "Back up, Rosa. Your crazy train mind is showing. You want financial freedom in your life? Then you better learn to trust me. If this comes down to someone wearing chains, it won't be me."

He walked past her without breaking eye contact, shut the door behind him, climbed into his Jeep, and drove back to the bungalow.

As he drove, Chad thought about how quickly he needed to finalize Rosa's setup. He knew this had to end soon, before Rosa tried to put him in chains instead.

Sophie barely crossed his mind anymore.

The real Chad was back in control.

* * *

By the end of the week, Chad believed everything was fine between him and Sophie. He had put plans into motion for her and Rosa as well, even though his resurfacing feelings for Sophie briefly made him wonder if he wanted to save her and keep her in his life.

Those thoughts did not last.

His narcissistic, sociopathic mind shut them down quickly as visions of the million dollar life insurance policy took over. Greed won, as it always did.

* * *

Chad woke early Saturday morning to prepare the bungalow for Sophie's arrival. He bought several bunches of flowers, plenty of candles, and her favorite wine, cheeses, and other indulgent treats. He wanted her wrapped in romance and ambiance, blind to the manipulation and control he believed would make his power over her irresistible.

Sophie pulled into the bungalow driveway an hour before noon.

Chad was ready with his charm and fake smile, prepared to proceed with his plan, completely unaware that Sophie's trap had already been set in place earlier that week.

She sat in the car for a moment, smiling devilishly as she imagined how neither Chad nor Rosa would see what was coming.

Inside her, something dark laughed.

This time, Sophie, you are not the prey. You are their executioner. Perfect revenge.

The bungalow smelled of sandalwood candles and salt air, their familiar ritual. Chad crossed the room, slipped his arms around her, and kissed her gently.

"I missed you so much, my beautiful woman."

Sophie looked at him lovingly, though her thoughts were cold. *You didn't miss me. You missed the insurance payout you and Rosa will never see.*

She pressed herself against him, her fingers trailing down his chest as she whispered, "We can show each other how much we missed us, now that we're both here in our love nest. Just us. Just like always."

Chad kissed her deeply, completely convinced.

Sophie returned the kiss with heat, even as her mind mapped the bungalow as a trap rather than a playground.

"I'm definitely hungry for you, babe," Chad said, pulling back slightly, "but I'm also hungry for food. I haven't eaten since yesterday. I need to refuel so I can pleasure you all afternoon."

She laughed softly. "Sounds like a plan. I really need food too. What would you like me to fix?"

He took her hand and kissed it. "Oh no, babe. I want to take you out. We could go across the street for our favorite Thai food."

She paused, then said, "I think we should go to the seafood restaurant on the beach."

It was expensive, and she decided she would take everything she could from him.

They returned a few hours later, full of food and drinks, each convinced they were manipulating the other. Chad grabbed the tequila and mixed them another round, figuring he could soften her further with alcohol and indulgence.

He handed her the glass and raised his own. "Here's to you, my sexy, beautiful lover. And here's to us and our bright, exciting future."

They clinked glasses.

Sophie slipped deeper into her performance, lowering her gaze as if sadness had suddenly claimed her. Chad tilted her chin up with his fingers.

"What's got you sad all of a sudden, my lover?" he asked.

She leaned into his touch, her eyes soft, her voice quiet. "I'm just scared. I don't want to lose you."

Her voice cracked perfectly.

"You'll never lose me, Sophie," he said, taking her face in both hands. "We're in this together. Always. Forever."

Rage thundered through her chest. She let a single tear fall and whispered, "Promise me, Chad. Promise."

He kissed her, sealing the lie.

Soon they were tangled together on the blankets on the floor, drinks forgotten. Sophie moaned his name, exaggerating every sound as Chad grew rough and dominant in his need.

Inside her mind, the demon purred.

Yes. Let him lose himself in you. Because when he is weakest, you will make sure he never rises again.

Chapter 29

The next morning, Sophie cooked breakfast for them. Bacon sizzled in the pan, eggs Benedict sat perfectly plated, and toast was buttered just right. Chad loved when she played house. It made him feel powerful, like he was the one in charge.

Sophie laughed silently to herself.

This son of a bitch has no idea I'm the one in charge. My power is stronger than his and Rosa's combined.

"You know," Sophie said casually as she sipped her coffee, "I was thinking about the insurance papers we signed. It really makes sense. I'm glad you convinced me to sign them. I want you protected, baby."

Chad froze mid bite, then slowly relaxed and smiled, relief flooding his face. "I want you protected too, sweetheart. I'm very happy you see how it makes sense for our future."

She nodded. "Of course. I love you too much not to."

Her demons laughed inside her head, whispering approval.

Yes. Let him believe it. Smile while you write his ending, and Rosa's too.

"You're so strong in every way, Chad," she whispered, resting her hand on his arm.

He grinned. "I love being strong for you. You bring it out in me, my sexy woman. You always have."

She kissed him slowly, lingering just long enough for her nails to graze his skin, hinting at possession. "Then don't ever let me go," she said softly.

Inside her mind, she rehearsed every step of her revenge.

You won't let go, she thought. *You'll never get the chance to hurt me. I'll take care of you both before either of you see me coming.*

"Stay with me one more night, my little sex machine," Chad said in his deep, almost demonic voice.

"Of course I will, baby," Sophie replied sweetly. "Anything for you."

She let him believe he had convinced her. His ego swelled, satisfied that he was still in control.

That evening, they sat together on the large swing on the deck. Sophie sipped her wine while Chad nursed a glass of bourbon. Suddenly, his phone rang.

Sophie caught the flicker of guilt in his eyes when he glanced at the screen. Rosa.

He looked up at Sophie, uncertain. She smiled sweetly and brushed her fingers over his hand. "Ignore it. Tonight is ours."

He kissed her, distracted, and she let him. In her mind, she was already writing the final chapter.

Rosa and Chad would never see their plan succeed.

Instead, Sophie would turn their world inside out while she walked away free and alive, leaving them pointing fingers at each other.

Whichever one survived, that is.

Chapter 30

During the next week, Sophie made excuses to Chad about why she could not stay at the bungalow the way she had before, assuring him she would be there over the weekend. While she did have work and patients to catch up on, she also had far more important matters to attend to. Her plans for revenge required time, precision, and secrecy.

She sensed that Chad and Rosa would try to get rid of her very soon so they could cash in on the insurance policy. Everything had to be in place. She needed to stay one step ahead of them.

I'll let them come close, she told herself. *Let them think I'm walking into their trap. They'll think I'm afraid. They'll think they've won. And they'll never see me.*

Sophie smiled, her hands trembling, not with fear but with excitement. The voice in her mind whispered approval, reminding her she already knew how to do this. This was perfect revenge.

* * *

One late evening, Chad stood at the glass doors of the bungalow, staring out at the dark stretch of water lapping gently against the dock. He turned sharply at the sound of the front door opening.

Rosa stood there.

"What the hell?" he yelled. "What if Sophie had been here? You can't just barge in whenever you want."

"Relax, Chad," she snapped. "I know when she's here and when she isn't."

She brushed past him and stepped out onto the deck. Then she turned back toward him, her expression sharp as she spoke quietly.

"Sophie needs to drown out there. It's clean. It's quick. No one will question it. People slip, people panic, and she'll just keep sinking until she drowns."

Chad leaned against the door, arms crossed, watching her with carefully controlled stillness. "You're certain that's the way?" he asked, his voice low and even.

He wanted her to believe he was weighing her plan, though his thoughts were already moving in another direction.

The night air was thick and humid as Rosa leaned toward him, her voice a venomous hiss. "No more playing house with your nurse, Chad. She drinks, she stumbles, and then she drowns. That's the end of it. It's that simple."

Chad pretended to sigh. "You really think drowning will be convincing? Accidents don't always convince people, Rosa," he said sharply. "If Sophie's body turns up floating near the bungalow, the police will ask questions."

"Trust me," Rosa snapped, rolling her eyes. "It'll look like an accident. You just need to stop hesitating." She stormed back into the bungalow, fury radiating from her. "We've talked enough, Chad. I want her gone. She dies in the water."

She jabbed a finger into his chest, her teeth clenched. **"No more excuses. No more delays. Sophie does not walk away from here alive."**

Chad reached for his glass of bourbon, masking his thoughts with a slow, measured sip. "If that's how you want it done, then that's how we'll do it," he said smoothly.

Outwardly, he looked compliant. Inside, his mind worked like a chessboard, calculating ten moves ahead.

Rosa thinks she's tightening the noose around me, he thought. *But I'm the one tightening it around her throat.*

He lifted his glass in her direction as she stormed out the door, her voice echoing behind her. "Get it done. Do you understand?

Chapter 31

By Wednesday night, Sophie had almost finished getting her plans for Chad and Rosa completed, leaving her a couple of days to finalize everything.

She had just poured herself a glass of wine when there was a knock at the door. It was too late for a neighbor or a delivery.

When she opened the door, her younger sister Samantha stood there in a rumpled jean jacket, road dust on her boots, and her auburn hair sticking up from long hours of driving. Sophie's mouth fell open in shock. Samantha grinned.

"Surprise, big Sis!"

Sophie gathered herself and blurted, "Sam? What the hell? What are you doing here?"

Sam pushed past her with that crooked grin. "You weren't answering my calls, so I figured I'd bring the conversation to your doorstep."

Sophie shut the door behind her, her stomach tightening. She had not expected to see her sister, not at this time, certainly not like this.

Samantha Monroe, Sam to family and friends, was a free-spirited, thrill-seeking freelance photographer and part-time bartender. She was charming when she wanted to be, but also had a sharp tongue and usually ran toward chaos rather than away from it. Sam was slim and wiry, her energy making her seem always on the move. She had grown up in the shadow of her older sister Sophie, who had always been responsible, studied hard, excelled in school, and tried to take care of her little sister. Sam was close to fifteen years younger than Sophie and had never liked the rules and bossiness Sophie tried to impose. She had rebelled through her teenage years, always making bad choices that Sophie had to bail her out of.

Despite the frustration, Sophie loved her little sister fiercely. A part of her felt she had to protect Sam from the world and sometimes even from herself. At the same time, Sam had a way of getting under Sophie's skin like no one else, irritating her enough to want to choke her.

Sophie took Sam's bags, scolding her as she said, "You drove from Colorado without telling me? You can't just show up here without letting me know."

Sam glared at her, eyes narrowing. "I called many times. You didn't respond. I just told you that. So save your lecture. If me driving here from Boulder and showing up unexpectedly is a problem, that's on you, big Sis."

The words hung in the air like smoke. Sophie's hand trembled as uneasiness rose through her body. She took a deep breath to calm herself, and her body relaxed as she smiled faintly and hugged Sam.

"I apologize. It's been a stressful time recently. It's late, and I guess I'm a little grumpy," Sophie said quietly.

"You're still my baby sister, no matter how much you drive me crazy. And you're right. Maybe I do push people away. I should have called you."

Sam softened a little, guilt flushing her face. "I didn't mean it like that," she said, managing a small smile. "You know I just thought you might need me this time."

Sophie laughed reluctantly. For a moment, the tension faded, even if the cracks remained.

She poured a glass of wine for Sam, thinking, *No matter the arguments, the disappointments, or the emotional tug-of-war, we always come back to each other.* Sam might scream that she didn't need anyone, but when her world fell apart, Sophie was always there to pick up the pieces.

Sophie was caught off guard by Sam's rare vulnerability. Sophie quietly said, "I always need you too. I'd do anything to protect you, and I know you'll be there for me."

Sam shrugged, brushing it off. "Just saying, you're still the bossy big sister I wanted to strangle half the time. But you're also the one I'd call if the world fell apart. And you know I'd burn it down for you, right?"

Her tone softened. "No, seriously. You've always had this strength, like nothing could break you. I know I am not easy, and I know I push your buttons. When everything went to hell, you held us together. You held me together."

Sophie managed a smile as she reached over and held Sam's hands.

Sophie worried about how she would handle her plans for revenge with Sam around. Her sister might stumble onto Chad and Rosa's schemes accidentally or even become a pawn in their manipulation. Sophie's protective instincts could flare dangerously if Sam's safety was threatened, pushing her deeper into her dark side.

No, she thought. *I have to get Sam out of here within a couple of days before she gets caught up in this web of deceit and murder.*

They talked and drank wine for a few more hours, catching up after not seeing each other for years. Sophie decided she would call in sick to work for the next couple of days, so she could spend time with Sam while finishing the last details of her plan and then convince her to return to Boulder.

Sophie showed Sam the guest bedroom and told her that she was off work tomorrow so they could spend time together. She planned to take Sam out to brunch in the morning, after which she could complete the remaining pieces of her plan for Chad and Rosa and figure out how to get Sam safely out of Jacksonville by Friday.

Over the next few days, the sisters enjoyed each other's company. Their conversations were full of laughter and shared memories. Sophie enjoyed the facade of normalcy, cooking together, watching old movies, and pretending the world hadn't become a tangle of lies and blood in her mind.

She kept the demons and the past at bay while completing the last details of her plan for Chad and Rosa. But she still had not figured out how to convince Sam to return to Colorado. She could not risk her little sister getting caught in the crosshairs of this situation or discovering what she had planned.

* * *

By Friday morning, Sophie felt stressed and anxious about her "company." *I have to get her out of here now,* she thought, fighting the demons whispering in her ear. *Get out of my head,* she screamed to herself.

A knock at her bedroom door brought her back to reality. "Hey Sophie, are you awake?" Sam called.

Sophie opened the door with a smile. "Of course! I'm surprised you're up and moving, though, considering how much we drank last night."

Sam laughed. "I took an aspirin when I went to bed. Keeps hangovers away. I did make coffee, though, in case you needed it."

"Great idea, thanks. I definitely need a cup," Sophie responded.

Sophie stood over the stove, spatula in hand, flipping the blueberry pancakes. She remembered how Sam liked them when she was young. She had made all her little sister's favorites, arranging her plate exactly how Sam liked it: scrambled eggs with cheese, crispy bacon, strawberries sliced in half, buttered toast, and pancakes in the center topped with blueberries and a little whipped cream.

Sam walked out of the bathroom, hair wet from the shower, wearing her Bohemian robe. She stopped as the smell hit her. "Oh my God, is that blueberry pancakes I smell? And bacon?" she squealed. "You haven't made this for me since... since you were yelling at me for stealing your lip gloss!"

Sophie smirked as she set the plate on the table. "Yeah, you broke the applicator. I was furious."

Sam sat down, eyes wide. "Holy crap... you even cut the toast into triangles! I swear you used to yell at me when I refused to eat it square," she giggled.

Sophie laughed, soft and genuine. "Well, I figured some habits die hard," she said as she handed her the maple syrup.

The sisters burst into laughter as they traded childhood stories about sneaking into the pantry late at night for snacks. Sam teased Sophie about her obsession with slipping their mother's romance novels into her backpack. Sophie fired back, reminding Sam of her embarrassing crush on the boy next door who had been far too old for her. Their laughter spilled over breakfast, and for a moment it felt as though the years between them had disappeared.

As Sam finished her food, she pushed her plate away. Her expression shifted as she leaned forward on her elbows.

"Thanks for breakfast. It was delicious, just like I remember from when we were younger," she said. "But you know I didn't come all this way just to eat pancakes and relive the good times."

Sophie's smile faltered as she slid her own plate aside. "Oh?" she asked lightly, avoiding her sister's gaze. "I figured nostalgia was good for the soul."

"It is," Sam replied, tilting her head as she studied Sophie closely. "But I know you. I know when you're locking something away. You're trying too hard, Sophie. All of this, the breakfast, the memories. You're pretending everything is fine. I can feel it, and you know I can." She took a slow breath. "You've been acting distant. Jumpy. Like you're preparing for something. It reminds me of before."

Sophie froze, her hand tightening around her coffee cup. "Before what?" she asked evenly.

Sam's voice softened. "Before the incident. The one you made me promise never to talk about. I didn't forget, Sophie. I can't keep pretending I don't see it. I know those shadows you're trying to keep buried. You think I don't feel them too? You know we're the same."

Sophie's chest tightened. She forced a brittle laugh. "You're imagining things, Sam. Have some more fruit."

But Sam's gaze stayed steady, sharp with both love and suspicion. "No. And you don't get to laugh this off anymore."

Sophie's smile faded. "You don't know what you're talking about. I'm just being myself."

"I know enough," Sam said quietly. "Enough to see you slipping into it again. Whatever this is," she added, gesturing toward Sophie, "it scares me, sis."

Sophie inhaled slowly, trying to steady the racing in her chest. She had hoped the pancakes and strawberries would distract Sam, soften the distance time had carved between them.

But Sam had always been sharper than she looked, more intuitive than Sophie wanted to admit. The sweetness of breakfast vanished, leaving behind the bitter taste of secrets dragged into the light.

"That's not fair," Sophie snapped. "You have no idea what's in my head. You promised not to bring that up."

"Fair?" Sam shot back. "Was it fair when you disappeared without a word all those years ago? You acted like everything was normal while it ate me alive inside."

Sophie stood, frustration rising. "I'm sorry you're dealing with stress and anxiety from that time. No one understands that better than I do. But maybe you should head back to Colorado. Today."

Sam shook her head. "And there it is. The dismissal. I'm not going anywhere until you admit something else is going on."

Sophie turned away, her chest tight. "I need to take a shower. We'll talk after."

While Sophie was in the bathroom, Sam wandered into her sister's bedroom. Her eyes caught on a notebook half-hidden beneath clothes on a chair. Curiosity tugged at her. She pulled it free and flipped through pages of scribbled notes. Medical terms. Dosages. References to life insurance policies.

Her confusion deepened. *If this is work-related, why is it hidden?* she wondered.

Back in the living room, she spotted Sophie's laptop bag. After glancing around, she opened it and quickly guessed the password. Inside was a folder labeled *Insurance and Contingency*.

Sam clicked it open.

Scanned insurance policies. Screenshots of text messages between two people named Chad and Rosa. And a document titled *Reversal Strategy*.

Her breath caught as she read. It outlined methods to manipulate evidence and frame Chad and Rosa for each other's murder.

"Oh my God," she whispered. "What has my sister done?"

Chapter 32

When Sophie returned, hair damp and a towel draped around her shoulders, she froze. Sam stood there holding the notebook, the laptop open beside her.

"You shouldn't have opened that," Sophie said calmly, her voice cold. "That's private."

Sam looked up, panic flashing across her face. "Sophie, what is this?" she demanded, holding up the notebook.

"Put it down."

"No." Sam's voice shook. "You've written a step-by-step plan to kill two people. Who are Chad and Rosa? This is not you. Please, not again."

Sophie lunged forward, snatching the notebook and slamming the laptop shut.

"Are you insane?" Sam shouted. "This isn't just notes. It's a blueprint for revenge."

Sophie paced, her hands trembling. "You don't understand."

"Then explain it," Sam snapped. "Because I know what you did years ago. I know what you've been hiding. If you don't tell me the truth, I'll have to tell someone."

The words struck like a blade. Sophie wanted to scream, to throw Sam out, but exhaustion and fear tangled inside her. Her voice wavered. "If I tell you, there's no going back. You'll see me as a monster. You won't be able to forget any of it."

Sam leaned closer. "I already know more than you think. And if you want me to stay quiet, you'd better start being honest."

"They're planning to drown me," Sophie said quietly. "They want the insurance money. I found out. I have to protect myself."

"Protecting yourself doesn't mean planning murder," Sam shot back. "You swore to heal people, not destroy them."

"They don't deserve my healing," Sophie replied bitterly. "This is about survival. It's the only way to beat them."

"By becoming like them?" Sam said. "This isn't who you are."

"Who I was won't survive what's coming," Sophie whispered. "So tell me, Sam. Should I just lie down and drown for them?"

The tension crackled between them, sister against sister. Sam fell silent, seeing something dark and unyielding in Sophie's eyes.

For the first time in years, Sophie felt the walls closing in. Sam was no longer the reckless kid sister. She had leverage now. And Sophie's buried past was clawing its way back to the surface, tangled with a present that threatened to destroy them both.

The air inside Sophie's apartment grew heavier with every word. They had argued for nearly an hour. Accusations. Justifications. Tears. Silence. Then Sam's voice cut through it all like a blade.

"I can't do this anymore, Sophie. This isn't you," she said, her voice breaking. "If you won't stop, I will go to the police. They need to know about Chad and Rosa's plan. And about what you're planning too. All of it needs to be stopped."

Sophie froze, her hands gripping the edge of the kitchen counter so tightly her knuckles went white.

"You wouldn't dare," she snapped.

Sophie paced the length of the room while Sam sat on the edge of the couch, arms wrapped around her knees.

"Don't test me," Sam said, her voice trembling but firm. "This isn't a debate anymore. You've gone too far, and it scares me. I won't stand here and watch my sister, my only family, turn into someone I don't recognize. I'm serious."

Sophie's chest heaved, her eyes shining with something caught between rage and grief. "You think the police will believe me? Now? You think they'll stop Chad? Or Rosa? They already decided my fate. They want me gone. If I don't act first, I'm dead. **Dead.**"

Sam swallowed hard, blinking back tears. When she spoke again, she forced herself to stay calm.

"Then maybe you should run. But I can't let you kill them. That isn't saving yourself, Sophie. That's crossing a line you can't uncross. Again."

Something inside Sophie fractured. Her voice dropped to a trembling whisper. "So you'd rather see me buried than have blood on my hands? You don't understand at all."

Sam stood, lifting her hands in a helpless, pleading gesture. "You can't do this. I don't care what you tell yourself. I have to stop you."

Sophie spun on her, her voice erupting. "You don't get to threaten me in my own home. Do you have any idea what they've done to me? The lies. The betrayal. The way they laughed behind my back while they planned my funeral?"

Sam's face twisted with pain as tears spilled down her cheeks. "And you think plotting their deaths will fix it? You're becoming just like them."

The words struck Sophie like a slap. Her throat tightened, tears burning despite the fury blazing in her eyes.

"Don't you dare compare me to them. I am not a monster. I'm a survivor. Everything I've done is to make sure I'm not the one dragged out of the water. **Not me**."

Sam reached for her hands, her voice soft and pleading. "Then let me help you in a different way. You can come to Boulder with me. They won't be able to hurt you there. But if you go through with this plan, I'll have no choice but to stop you, even if that means turning you in."

Sophie tore her hands free, her entire body shaking with betrayal.

"You'd betray me?" she nearly screamed. "After everything we survived together? After Mom, after Dad, after all the nights I held you while you cried? And now you'd hand me over to the wolves?"

Sam's eyes glistened, but her jaw remained set.

Sophie moved quickly into her bedroom and returned just as fast.

Sam stepped toward the door, as if preparing to leave. Sophie acted before she could think about how far she was willing to go. She held something in one hand as she grabbed Sam with the other, driven by nothing but the need to stop her sister from walking out.

"Sophie, you're hurting me. This is wrong. Let me go," Sam cried.

Sophie dragged her into the guest bathroom and snapped a handcuff around her wrist, securing the other cuff to a metal rack bolted into the wall. Sam jerked against the restraint, her eyes rimmed red with fear and fury.

"You can't be serious. You're actually going to lock me in here? Sophie, stop this now," she pleaded.

The bathroom smelled of lavender. It sat in the center of the apartment with no windows, and now it served as a cell.

"I know," Sophie said hoarsely. "I'm so sorry. I'm truly sorry, Sam."

She pressed her palms to her temples, as if she could force the panic back inside. Her voice came out low and brittle. "I didn't want this. I told you I didn't want to do this, but you left me no choice. If you go to the police, they'll..."

"They'll what?" Sam interrupted, her voice shaking. "Believe Chad? Arrest you? Sophie, this is insane. You're the one who's going to get hurt. Or worse."

Terror clenched Sophie's chest, but she forced herself to breathe.

"I'm not expecting you to understand. It's obvious that you don't. I'm just asking you to trust me for a few days and stay here. I promise when I get back, we'll talk about everything."

"Trust you?" Sam snapped. "You want me to trust you while you go off to murder two people, or end up dead instead?"

The words cut like ice. Sophie shook her head, furious, exhausted, and afraid. "Sam, please. Just give me a few days. If I come back," her voice broke, "when I come back, I'll face whatever happens."

Sam let out a sharp, bitter laugh. "And what if you don't come back? What if they get you first? What happens to me?"

The question lodged inside Sophie like rot. She saw two futures clearly. One where she waited and was destroyed. One where she acted and everything changed forever. Both terrified her.

"I promise you I'll come back," she said quietly. "I'll handle this, and then we'll figure it out together."

"Promises don't mean anything anymore, Sophie," Sam said softly as she sat on the toilet.

Sophie moved before she could stop herself. She rushed to the kitchen and gathered bottles of water, a sandwich, and whatever food she could find. She packed ice packs into a cooler with the supplies.

Sam's voice echoed through the apartment as she shouted Sophie's name and pounded on the walls. With the bathroom door closed, the sound was already muffled.

Sophie pushed the cooler inside with a pillow and blanket on top.

She locked the door and pressed a thick blanket along the bottom to dampen the sound. For now, all she knew was that she needed time to set the plan in motion at the bungalow.

Sam's muffled cries made Sophie's chest ache. She leaned her forehead against the door, listening.

"You're making a mistake. This isn't you. Please, Sophie," Sam begged.

"I love you more than anything," Sophie whispered through the door. "But I have to stop these two demons."

Then she walked away.

Chapter 33

Outside, the humidity of Jacksonville closed around her like a shroud. The bungalow awaited.

Every step toward Chad and Rosa felt like moving deeper into a storm. As she drove away, Sophie's hands trembled on the steering wheel, not from fear of being caught, but from the image of Sam alone in that room. Betrayed. Frightened. Silenced.

All because Sophie had convinced herself there was no other way.

The drive to the bungalow was mostly silent. Sophie turned on the radio to calm her nerves. She thought about conversations with Chad - the words, the betrayals he had set up for her to believe.

Suddenly, her stomach twisted as if she were going to be sick. It wasn't hunger, and not even remorse; it was just the understanding that there would be no undoing what she was going to do.

Sophie parked down the road and walked up to the bungalow, slipping around back and unlocking the glass door off the deck. She didn't want to be seen going through the front door in the middle of the afternoon.

She walked through the bungalow with careful steps and sharp eyes.

She needed to make sure a few things were put in place before tomorrow, the day she was to be murdered by Chad and Rosa. But she wasn't going to let that happen because the tables would be turned on them, she thought as she put on plastic gloves from her office.

Sophie checked drawers, cabinets, closets, and everywhere else she could think of. She wanted to see if they had any traps, evidence, or even weapons in place for her demise. This way, she could stay a step ahead of Chad and Rosa.

She didn't find anything, though; she thought maybe they were waiting until that night, since Chad knew she wasn't coming over until the next day.

Finally, Sophie moved to the bedroom and opened the drawer where the life insurance policies were. She picked up the folder and replaced it with one from her bag. They looked exactly alike.

"Great," she thought. "Almost everything's in place."

She looked around the room, thinking she was hearing a humming. She realized it was a slow, precise noise of rationale, not of violence, but implication. She imagined the aftermath, feeling both triumphant and empty.

Victory, she told herself, that was what she would tell herself later too. It had nothing to do with violence; it had everything to do with making the truth visible, especially to Sam.

She left the bungalow the same way she had arrived, and there was no evidence she had been there. Even all her fingerprints had been wiped from their "love nest."

She walked back to her Mercedes, quietly quoting something a friend had said to her: *Bad things happen to good people... and good things happen to bad people! But vengeance is mine, sayeth the Lord!*

This time, *vengeance was hers*, Sophie thought to herself.

About an hour later, Chad arrived and walked into the bungalow. He grabbed a drink and went out on the deck while he waited for Rosa. He heard her SUV pull into the driveway and instantly tensed as he tried to keep his poker face on.

Rosa entered the bungalow, seeing him on the deck. She very loudly said, "Looking at your little girlfriend's watery grave?"

Chad took a deep breath to stay calm, although inside he pictured his hands wrapped around Rosa's throat.

"Just thinking how the plan will play out," he said quietly.

Rosa stopped and laughed.

"Chad, you say that as if you still have feelings for poor little blondie."

She laughed again but whispered, "You have no idea how much I can take from you. You've always been good at pretending you don't know how ugly you sound when you lie!"

Chad's eyes flashed with something colder than charm; impatience, entitlement.

"Don't make this about Sophie," he said. "I'm trying to save us, the kids, the house, the money. Don't make me out to be a monster trying to drag us down, because you're the one that's going to look guilty. They'll wrap this up around you!"

Rosa's laughter changed to aggravation.

"No, they won't! And don't think you're going to pin this on me... I'll take you down first."

Chad took a step forward.

"Listen to me. People will look at you; they'll say you were jealous and lost control," he said softly. "That's just normal. You're better at playing a jealous spouse than I am... because frankly, I don't care about your sexcapades!"

Her laughter was hard and bitter.

"Nobody would think that's normal... we're not normal anymore. We used to be decent, Chad. Remember? At least I used to be decent."

Chad's jaw tightened with a near-perfect smile.

"I am decent, but I'm also realistic. Sophie's the obstacle, and once she's gone, the policy becomes our financial future."

He leaned toward her and said softly,

"You need to make this scene believable; you'll need to act like you love me this weekend. They'll believe what you make them believe."

Rosa looked at him for a long moment, as if trying to figure out exactly what he was up to.

"And you?" she said quietly. "What will you tell yourself when it's all said and done?"

Chad put on his fake smile.

"That it was necessary. That I did what I had to... for us."

"I don't want to go to prison, Chad. I want the money and my freedom. You better make sure I'm safe from that... because you're the one they'll look at too, I'll make sure of that!" Rosa raged as she stood up.

Tension boiled between them as she stormed out, shouting loudly.

Voices were raised, emotions raw, as their secrets came to the surface. Chad's expression brightened in a way that chilled her. He grabbed her arm, then let go as if he were afraid of his own temper. She glared, then looked at her arm and fiercely said,

"That's the last time you'll ever touch me, you son of a bitch!"

As he started to step toward her, he stopped, realizing there were people on the street staring at them. He calmed himself and quickly stepped back inside as Rosa got in her SUV and sped away.

Chapter 34

"It will play out like a scene in a movie, applause at the end because my bank account will be full," he said outloud.

Inside his smile was that of a narcissistic demon as he thought to himself, *This is perfect. I have her thinking the investigation will show the evidence points back to her.*

That was the hook he needed, because he knew Rosa would lose it and basically stamp her name on the drowning. She would go to prison, he would cash Sophie's life insurance policy, and he would take his boys and move into a luxurious life.

* * *

Sophie was parked down the road as Rosa sped by. She smiled fiendishly as she thought of her floating in the water behind the bungalow.

"Sophie, what are you doing?" she heard Sam's voice in her head. The small, hard laugh of the demon inside her took over the noise in Sophie's head.

We'll see who survives this. You're not a monster... you're a survivor.

She started her Mercedes and drove down the road past the bungalow, into another driveway.

* * *

Saturday unfolded as Sophie awoke to sounds of a distant siren and a woman shouting across the road. She stood up to look out the window and saw Chad's Jeep at the bungalow down the street.

She hadn't slept much the night before, but her mind was clear and sure of what had to be done that day.

She put on some coffee and jumped into the shower. As Sophie dressed, she went over the day's events in her head.

"This day will be perfect, successful, but most of all... satisfying!" she thought.

She gathered her things together, going over in her head the list of items for today's events.

She looked at the time, 11:11, and knew the clock was now ticking down to go time. She finished her coffee and wrote a note, leaving it on the kitchen counter.

Thanks for use of your place, perfect hideout in plain sight. Thanks again for all your help with everything, I'll see you in a few days. I WILL PREVAIL! -S

As Sophie gathered her bag and walked into the bungalow, Chad greeted her with a big smile and a kiss. He pulled back, looked her up and down, and exclaimed, "DAMN baby! You look like a million dollars. That bathing suit is so hot on you, is it new?"

Sophie acted like she was blushing and coy on the outside while inside she was thinking, *You think I look like a million dollars, huh? Guess who's taking that million dollars??*

"Ah honey, that's so sweet and sexy of you to say that," she said with her fake smile. "I thought we might go to the beach in a little while. I think I want a glass of wine right now. Do you want something honey?"

Chad was still looking at her, almost lustfully, as he replied, "Sure baby. I guess I'll have a glass of bourbon. You look different with your hair in a bun, the big hat and sunglasses that you had on when you walked in too."

Sophie never looked up as she responded, "Oh you can never be too protected from the sun. I thought they would be perfect for the beach."

She walked out on the deck with her glass of wine, Chad following her. She sat down on the dock, something she never did, and Chad looked confused.

"Well, this is different too. I've never seen you sit on the edge of the deck before."

He sat down beside her, hanging his feet in the water. Sophie started making small talk about work, the weather, and other meaningless things. Chad gulped his bourbon down and asked, "What's wrong, my baby? Did something happen?"

She realized she had not been very affectionate or attentive to him.

So she looked over and smiled, saying, "I'm sorry honey. It's been a rough week. One of my patients that I was very close to passed away this week. I'm just not good at processing these things sometimes."

She leaned over quickly, kissed him, and rested her head on his shoulder and chest.

After a few minutes, Sophie jumped up and said, "I'm going to have another glass of wine before we head to the beach. Here, let me get you some more bourbon, baby."

Chad started to get up. "Let me help you, sexy lady."

Sophie pushed him back down on the deck and said quickly, "No honey. Stay here. I want to wait on you. I have to take care of my man, right?"

She knew that would play right to Chad's ego, and she was right. He smiled smugly and said, "Well alright then. Bring me another, serving wench!"

She smiled, turned around, and fumed all the way back inside.

Sophie kept looking his way as she grabbed her bag and walked into the kitchen. She quickly poured more bourbon into his glass. Looking out the glass doors, she pulled a syringe out of the bag. She put just enough of the fentanyl into the bourbon to knock him out for several hours. She knew exactly the right dose. After all, she was a nurse.

She mixed his bourbon, poured herself some wine, and went back outside so Chad would not come looking for her.

"Here, sweet man, just as you like it, strong with one ice cube," she said as she kissed him.

Chad took a big gulp and smiled devilishly. "You have been the best thing that's come into my life. I'm so blessed and don't deserve you," he said, guilt thick in his voice.

Sophie gave him a look like she believed every piece of bullshit coming out of his mouth.

"We're very blessed, my dear. Here's to us!" she said, clinking his glass.

Chad winked and took another big gulp of bourbon. Sophie kept feeding his ego with flattering remarks and light touches of her fingers against his skin. She needed to make sure he drank the entire glass of bourbon with its twist of fentanyl.

As Chad stood up from the deck floor, he wobbled, and Sophie caught his arm to steady him.

"Whoa. I guess I had a little too much to drink. I did have a couple of glasses before you got here," Chad said, slurring slightly.

Sophie helped him over to the big swing on the deck.

"Here sweetie, sit down and rest. Just relax and it will be ok real soon," she said softly.

She knew he would be unconscious very soon, and then the rest of her plan would fall into place. Anxiety surged, and panic shot through her.

I can't do this, she thought.

The demons inside whispered back, *Yes you can. You've done it before. You've killed before. It will be quick and painless.*

Sophie moved quickly once Chad passed out. She put on the plastic gloves and began picking up everything she had touched so she could wipe her fingerprints and DNA from the scene.

She did not think about the how. She thought about the why. Chad's lies. Rosa's plan for the drowning. The million-dollar life insurance policy. Everything was set for their surprise.

Now it was time to get Rosa there.

She grabbed Chad's phone and sent a text.

C: I need you to come over now. It's urgent, I need your help with a situation.

Sophie smiled to herself. *That should get the bitch here very soon.*

She put everything in place for Rosa's arrival.

The bungalow was silent except for the faint hum of the ceiling fan. Sophie stood hidden in the corner behind the door, her hands gloved, the syringe tucked into her pocket. Chad's phone rested on the table as proof of the bait. Chad's texts to Rosa.

The front door opened, and Rosa stepped inside.

"Chad? Where is she?" Rosa whispered.

Sophie moved like a shadow, slipping behind Rosa before she could take another step.

She clamped one hand over Rosa's mouth while her other arm wrapped tightly around her chest and arms. Rosa thrashed, muffled words spilling against Sophie's palm.

"Shhh. It's me. The woman you thought you could drown like a stray animal," Sophie said in a low, controlled voice.

Rosa froze, panic widening her eyes.

Sophie leaned close to her ear and whispered, "You and Chad thought you were clever, but I'm the one who's been a step ahead of you. I know everything. The insurance deal. The drowning. You thought you could erase me, use me as **YOUR** meal ticket? I'm not the one disappearing tonight!"

Rosa struggled to speak. Sophie loosened her grip slightly, careful not to give her the chance to scream.

"You don't understand. Chad made me do this," Rosa pleaded.

Sophie tightened her hand again and said sharply, "No Rosa, you wanted it as much as him. I saw the texts between you. In fact, drowning me was your idea. And now you'll both get what you deserve!"

Rosa tried to scream and wrench free.

"Don't worry Rosa. It'll be quick. Just like you planned for me!"

In one swift motion, Sophie pulled the syringe from her pocket and plunged it into Rosa's arm before she could cry out. Rosa's eyes widened as the fentanyl hit her bloodstream. Sophie caught her as her body went limp and lowered her gently onto the couch.

"Sweet dreams, Rosa. When they find you, Chad won't know what hit him as they pull YOUR body from the watery grave."

Sophie straightened, her expression cold and certain. The pieces were falling into place. No longer the prey, she was writing the ending herself.

Time to finish it.

Chapter 35

A few hours had passed into late Saturday afternoon as Chad began to awaken. He was propped up on the big swing as he looked around, his eyes having a hard time focusing.

As he rubbed his eyes, his mind felt confused and foggy. His limbs felt heavy, and for a moment he thought he was still dreaming.

When he was finally able to stand, he tried to walk on the deck even though his legs were still wobbly. Suddenly, something caught his eye at the end of the deck.

His eyes widened, and he began to move faster toward the water. He gasped and almost screamed as he fell to his knees at the end of the deck.

Her body floated in the water, bobbing up and down in the bathing suit and hat that he remembered Sophie wearing earlier. He grabbed her arm and shoulders to try to pull her out of the water. The hat fell off, and her head fell back, exposing her face.

Chad dropped her body, and it fell back into the water as he let out a yell. "Oh my God, what the...?" he yelled as he saw Rosa's face, pale and very still.

He fell back on the deck, grabbed the railing, and inched backward away from the body.

"No, no, no, no!" Chad's voice cracked. "It wasn't supposed to be you, Rosa! Damn it!" His breath came in shallow gasps. "This... this isn't right. Think Chad, think. Sophie was supposed to..." His voice trailed off into a broken sob.

His thoughts tangled in panic. He had no plan for this. No cover story. Nothing. "No, no, no," he screamed, clutching his head. "This isn't happening!"

A neighbor's voice called out from across the fence of another bungalow, "Hey, everything ok over there? What's going on?"

Chad froze. Calming himself, he stood up and backed slowly toward the bungalow. It was too late. His cries had betrayed him. Looking back at Rosa's body still in the water, his stomach turned. He couldn't drag her out. How would he explain this?

In a very short time, he heard sirens. Then he saw flashing blue and red lights pull up in front of the bungalow. The knock at the door was firm as a voice called out, "Jacksonville Sheriff's Dept. Open up."

Chad stumbled back inside, sweat beading at his temples. His voice quivered as he muttered, "Oh God, they can't see this, they can't know."

The knock came again, louder, and he realized the choice was gone. He was trapped in this nightmare. *Had Sophie set him up?* he wondered. *Where is she?*

* * *

The bungalow was now a scene of several Jacksonville Sheriff's vehicles as well as the hulking presence of the coroner's van at the edge of the driveway. Chad was inside, pacing like a man trying to remember how to breathe, his face scared and boyish.

"Were you and the victim the only ones here today, sir?" the officer asked Chad. His hands made a wild, useless shape of someone reaching for explanation.

"I don't, I don't know," he said, clenching his jaw. "But I didn't..." The rest of the words cracked off into a sound that could be grief or maybe fear.

A pocket of hysterical composure collapsed in on Chad. He kept repeating the same sentences.

"I don't know how this happened, it wasn't supposed to be this way, I swear!" Each repetition made him sound less like a man who hadn't done it and more like a man trapped in a script he couldn't rewrite.

Sophie folded her arms against the September wind as she watched it all unfold from the safety of the bungalow down the street. Her car was hidden close to the backside of her friend's place.

She watched with binoculars out of the window so she could see Chad and the police inside their bungalow. She enjoyed seeing him being reduced to the pathetic narcissist she realized he had always been. She had not touched him, she had not confronted him, but she had tilted the scales in her favor and blown his world apart.

She watched the deputies move through the bungalow like careful predators, opening drawers and peering under cushions. She thought about how all this would become headlines by tomorrow, realizing that the horrific plan they had started consumed them to their fate. Sophie smiled wickedly.

Neighbors had begun to gather together as close to the bungalow as they were allowed. She wanted to move closer so she could hear what the neighbors were saying and maybe see a little better inside the bungalow.

She threw on some reading glasses, pulled her hair up, and covered it with a cap to disguise herself. She stood behind the bystanders as she listened to their conversations.

One of the neighbors decided to make herself a witness as she motioned to the deputy standing in the driveway. "Officer? Was it the blonde woman that died?"

The officer stepped toward the woman and said, "It's an ongoing investigation, ma'am. Right now, we're just following where the evidence points. Did you see or hear anything?"

Sophie's stomach turned when she heard the mention of a blonde woman. Rosa could pass for blonde, she thought, but not as blonde as she was. Sophie pulled the cap down tighter and made sure her hair was covered. People sometimes talk into silences like they can fill them.

The neighbor offered testimony about seeing a blonde woman here many times, overhearing voices and arguments from the night before, and an account of an SUV leaving late the night before. And now Rosa's SUV was back in the driveway today. *Couldn't have planned it more perfectly myself,* thought Sophie.

Sophie was trying to find a way to move closer when the door of the bungalow opened and the coroner's people wheeled out a filled body bag.

Sophie's heart skipped a beat as the picture in her head showed how she put Rosa's body in the water, pushing her head under. Rosa's eyes had peeked open, then widened as she started struggling. Sophie was able to hold her under the water since Rosa was weak from the fentanyl. It didn't take long for Rosa's struggle to slow down, her eyes closing as she drowned.

Sophie brought herself back to reality as the coroner's van pulled away.

The deputy inside continued to question Chad about events from last night through today. He asked the same questions several times, trying to see if the answers were consistent. Chad grew frustrated; he was confused from the fentanyl and all the bourbon he had drunk. His head was pounding as he tried to think about the questions he was being asked.

"Sir, can you tell me what happened last night?" the officer asked. Chad's brain was scrambled, unable to establish timelines in his mind.

"We had an argument, she left. I was trying to clear my head. I think. I don't know after that," he said quietly.

"So, let me get this straight. She was here last night with you, she left, and did she come back last night or sometime this morning?" the officer asked again.

Chad's voice raised loudly. "I told you already. I don't remember anything after she left last night. I woke up a while ago and I saw her in the water. I don't know anything else!"

"Well, it seems you were the last one to see her alive, huh?" the officer said.

The crime scene was a chorus of voices, uniformed officers combing the deck, divers in and out of the water. The body had long since been taken away, but the deputies lingered methodically, as if unwilling to let the bungalow give up its secrets too quickly.

The detective questioned Chad over and over as he sat slumped at the table, his head in his hands.

The detective closed his notebook and said bluntly, "Mr. Thornton, your statements aren't adding up. You've contradicted yourself several times. You say you were asleep, then woke up on a chair on the deck and saw the victim's body in the water. There are bruise marks on her arms, and your fingerprints are on everything that are hers. These things don't happen from slipping. Your wife didn't just fall."

Chad lifted his head as his face drained of color. "You don't know what you're talking about. I didn't touch her! I don't know when she got here or how," he said loudly and angrily.

The detective held up an evidence bag with the insurance folder in it. "This is a good piece of evidence for her murder. You recently took out an insurance policy on her for a million dollars."

He nodded toward the other deputy as he said to Chad, "Enough. We're done here. Cuff him. Mr. Thornton, you're being arrested for the murder of Rosa Thornton."

The scrape of the chair legs echoed as Chad was pulled to his feet, his wrists forced behind his back. He thrashed about as the steel locked around his wrists.

"This is insane! You're making a mistake!" he yelled. "It's a set up. Somebody set me up!"

Outside the bungalow, Sophie stood back and watched from the shadows of the bystanders, her arms folded across her chest. Chad's head was down as the officer led him to the patrol vehicle, his eyes glancing around at the crowd. He thought he caught a glimpse of someone that looked like Sophie as he was put in the vehicle.

Sophie looked at him. He looked smaller than she had ever seen him.

For the first time in months, Sophie's shoulders loosened, and the pressure in her chest released. The vindication was sweeter than she imagined. It wasn't just Rosa gone; it was Chad stripped of his power. Her lips curled into a thin smile as she thought, *So much for your plans, Chad.*

As the door of the patrol vehicle slammed shut, she whispered to herself, "Checkmate."

She turned on her heel, heading back to her car, her heart pounding but not from fear, rather from satisfaction. It was time to leave the chaos behind and return to her apartment where Sam was waiting and needed to be handled. Sophie knew their unfinished conversation would be the next storm to weather.

Chapter 36

Sophie slipped her key into the lock, her hands trembling. The apartment was dark except for the faint glow of the bathroom light beneath the door. She swallowed hard, her throat dry. "Sam," she called out softly from outside the bathroom.

"You came back," Sam said with a raspy voice from yelling all the time Sophie was gone. "Did you do it, Sophie? Did you kill them?"

As she unlocked the bathroom door, she saw Sam sitting on the edge of the bathtub, her wrist still cuffed, and her face stained from tears.

"How could you? You actually went through with it, didn't you?" Sam exclaimed with red eyes and tears.

Sophie lowered her gaze. "It's finished, Sam. Everything's over. We don't have to worry about Chad and Rosa ever again. They'll never hurt me again. I did what I had to do. We can move on, Sam."

Sam let out a bitter laugh. "Move on? You're no better than them. You're worse!"

Sophie said firmly, "Stop. You don't understand. I need you to just go along with me on this. Stop trying to be in charge for one minute. I had no choice."

Sam shook her head violently, her voice cracking as she yelled, "No! You CHOSE to do it. Don't twist this into some noble act. You're a killer, Sophie. And you locked me up like some animal while you went and did it!"

Sophie's composure cracked, her voice raw. "I did it for us. For you, for me, so we could finally be free of what they had planned to do."

Sam's eyes blazed as she said through clenched teeth, "Don't you dare put this on me. I would rather die than live with what you've done AGAIN!"

Sam's voice was hoarse but stern. "Uncuff me and let me out this instant!"

The words struck Sophie like a blade, but she reached to free Sam's wrist from the handcuff. "I had to keep you safe. You would've ruined everything," she said as she looked at Sam.

She yanked her hand free and said angrily, "Safe? You don't even know what the word means anymore."

The tension was so thick Sophie could barely breathe. "I'm your big sister," she pleaded. "It's done. We just... we just put it in the past, and no one needs to know."

Sam's voice rose. "Put it in the past? You killed somebody, Sophie! You can't bury this like you buried something else. Remember?"

Sophie begged, "Sam please."

Sam shoved past her, storming into the living room. Sophie caught her arm to stop her from leaving, and Sam spun around, rage coursing through her.

She jerked her arm away, stepping back from Sophie. Sam caught her foot on the edge of the big rug, fell backward, and before Sophie could catch her, Sam's skull collided with the corner of the coffee table.

The sound was final. "Sam!" Sophie screamed as she dropped to her knees and cradled her sister's head. Blood trickled down Sam's head, her eyes already glassy and fixed. She shook her, but Sam didn't move as Sophie tried to see if she was breathing. No breath came.

"No, no, please not you. I didn't mean for this to happen."

As Sophie sobbed through sharp gasps, she rocked back and forth, her chest heaving. The apartment spun around her. "I didn't mean – God, Sam, I didn't mean for this to happen."

She pressed her forehead to her sister's as her tears soaked into Sam's hair.

The irony seared into her. She had fought so hard to rid herself of Rosa and Chad's darkness only to have it destroy the one person she was trying to protect. Her apartment felt like a tomb.

For the first time, Sophie felt utterly powerless. She moved and softly laid Sam's head on the blood-soaked rug. She stepped back and looked at Sam's limp body. It was surreal, and suddenly she felt woozy.

She looked down at her own hands with sadness as she thought, *Isn't this ironic. I definitely have blood on my hands.*

She stood straight up, wiped her face with her shirt, and walked quickly to her bathroom. She knew she had to think and move quickly as she jumped in the shower.

Sophie quickly dressed in black clothes when she got out of the shower. She walked into the living room, catching her breath as she looked at her little sister lying in a pool of blood. *She looks so small and innocent,* thought Sophie.

She cleared her throat, wiped her tears away, and with gloved hands began to roll Sam in the rug. She was able to get her body in the trunk of her Mercedes without anyone seeing her. The night was dark with clouds and no moon, which made it easier for Sophie to take care of this issue.

She drove to a remote area of Jacksonville that would be perfect for her to dispose of Sam's body without anyone finding it. She and Chad

had found this place one time when they were exploring and enjoying each other's company.

I guess this was one good thing that came out of my time with the narcissistic bastard, she thought.

She dug a hole deep enough to keep wildlife from digging it up, put Sam in, and covered her with dirt. Sophie said a prayer as she wept, then headed back to her apartment.

* * *

At her apartment, she gathered her clothes and all of her personal items, packing the Mercedes until it was full. She checked everywhere to get all of Sam's things out as well.

Sophie had given her notice to the apartment personnel about a month ago when she had put her plans for Chad and Rosa in place. She had also given a month notice at work.

She rechecked the apartment one last time to make sure all the blood was cleaned up and nothing was left behind. She got in the car and drove to her friend's bungalow to stay for the night.

When she arrived, Ethan's truck was already there.

Chapter 37

Ethan MacKenzie was a former forensic crime scene technician, retired from the FBI. He now worked discreetly in private IT/AI security and surveillance consulting. He was tall, lean, good-looking with dark hair and piercing blue eyes. Ethan had met Sophie many years ago when she worked in the ER in a San Francisco hospital. She had treated him after a bar fight he had stumbled into, and their connection kept them in touch with each other.

Ethan had been extremely loyal to Sophie ever since then, and he was the one she contacted every time something happened. He assisted her in altering the insurance papers by forging dates, signatures, and digital files, as well as scrubbing Sophie's texts from Chad's phone. He used his forensic expertise to scrub Sophie's fingerprints and DNA from the bungalow and taught her how to stay two steps ahead of Chad and Rosa with tactical moves.

Sophie sat at the table in the bungalow with Ethan. The Florida night was thick, cicadas buzzing in the distance.

"You know you saved my life as you've done before. I don't know what I would have done without you and your expertise," Sophie said with a smile. "I don't know why you keep coming to my rescue. You've never told me. Why do you help me? Why risk yourself?"

Ethan leaned back in the chair as he explained, "Because once, a long time ago, I let someone die. I cleaned it up, buried them, and pretended it never happened."

He took a breath and softly said to her, "You're the first person who didn't ask me for excuses. You asked me for help. I knew from the first time we met in the ER that you're a good person, Sophie. You know I always say: *Bad things happen to good people and good things happen to bad people.*'

Sophie blinked, realizing the full weight of who he was.

Ethan slid a manila folder across the kitchen table to Sophie. She looked down at it, then stared back at him, not sure what it was.

Ethan tapped the folder with one finger as he said, "I've forged Rosa's digital consent, tweaked the time stamp, and changed the beneficiary from Chad to you. Whoever drafted the documents to begin with was very sloppy and thought no one would ever look twice.

But don't worry, I can redirect the payment to you without raising a flag. It's your decision. You just let me know."

Sophie took the documents, stood up, and gave Ethan a huge hug. "I can't thank you enough for all you do for me. You're my rock, Ethan," she said.

As she held up the folder, she winked and softly said, "I'll let you know about this. I'm going to lay down and rest before I leave in the morning."

Ethan smiled back and replied, "Be safe out there, my friend. I'll be gone before you wake. Until the next time." He held her and kissed her forehead as they said good night.

Chapter 38

The fluorescent hum of the jail corridor was muffled under the cloak of silence. Sophie decided to pay one last visit to Chad in jail before she left the city of Jacksonville.

Before Ethan left the bungalow in the early hours before dawn, Sophie had asked for help with one more thing. He had used his skills to plunge the corridor where Chad was being held into semi-darkness, giving Sophie just enough cover to slip through.

Ethan's IT skills allowed him to alter the camera's picture to show only Chad in his cell. Inside the cell, Chad sat slumped on the bunk, his face very pale.

Sophie stepped out of the shadows as she walked toward the cell. Chad's head snapped up, his whole body lit up like a child at Christmas.

"Sophie! Oh, thank God. I knew you'd come," he said with excitement. "Please, you've got to help me. Tell them I didn't do this to Rosa."

Sophie stepped closer but kept her face still. "I didn't kill her! She fell, you know that. You have to tell them!" Chad pleaded.

"You look scared, Chad. That's new," Sophie said calmly.

"Of course I'm scared! They think I drown Rosa, but it was an accident. Please get me out of here. I promise I can fix everything else," he begged.

Sophie tilted her head, her eyes steady and unblinking. "You sound desperate, Chad. That doesn't suit you. Where's the confident Navy Chief? Where's the man who thought he could manipulate me? The man who thought he and his wife could win?"

Chad blinked, confusion running through him. "What, what are you talking about?"

Sophie's eyes were almost glowing red as she replied, "You're right about one thing. Rosa drowned. But it wasn't an accident. I made sure of that. Every step, every detail, I placed it all in motion. You played your part quite well."

Chad froze, his breath catching. "What are you saying? Sophie, I don't understand. I thought you were here to save me."

Sophie's smile curled, faint but cruel.

"Save you? No, Chad. I came to say goodbye. You thought you had me trapped, didn't you? Rosa thought the same, but now she's gone. I put her in the water and made sure she never came back up. I left just enough behind so the police would see you as the perfect suspect. She's gone, you're here, and the world thinks you killed her."

The blood drained from his face.

Chad gripped the bars of his cell, his voice cracking. "No, no, you couldn't. You wouldn't do that."

Sophie took a slow step back, her eyes locked on his.

"I would, I did. And you know what the best part is? Everyone believes it. The great Chad Thornton brought down by his own lies. You'll stay in this cage begging for someone to believe you, while I walk free out there," she said as she pointed to the outside.

Chad's face twisted, half terror, half disbelief. "You set me up? You set me up!" he yelled.

Sophie leaned in, her voice a whisper sharp as glass. "I'll never be your victim again. You'll rot in here and I'll be free. That's justice, Chad. MINE!"

She slipped back into the shadows and down the corridor as she heard Chad yelling, "Sophie, please. Please don't do this. Don't leave me here. They're gonna bury me in here."

* * *

Sophie sat in her car in the far corner of the beach parking lot, the hum of the engine vibrating faintly under her hands. She had gone into the jail, faced Chad, and watched the panic uncoil in his face as he realized what she had done. She felt victorious but with a heavy chest.

You've always been good at wearing masks, the demon in her head whispered, sharp as glass. *The nurse. The healer. The sister. The lover. And now the executioner. How many roles will you play before you see what you really are?*

Sophie pressed her forehead against the steering wheel. Rosa had it coming. Chad deserved worse. They built the trap. She only sprung it.

Another voice in her head said, *You said the other one was the last, wasn't that what you told yourself back then? But here we are. Blood still clings to you, no matter how much you scrub.*

Her hands trembled. She had survived her past and now she had survived this. Her grip tightened on the wheel. It was over. It was finished. But the voices laughed in unison. *It's never finished. You didn't just end them. You stitched yourself tighter in this web. Guilt isn't a chain you can cut loose, Sophie. It's part of you, grows with you. When the time comes, it will strangle you.*

She looked in the rear-view mirror and gazed at her reflection. She pushed the demon voices down deep in her mind as a smile slowly crept in the reflection. **"I am Sophie Monroe, the survivor, the sinner, the avenger!"** she exclaimed loudly.

All three would follow her wherever she went.

Chapter 39

Sophie stood outside her car, staring out over the choppy waters of the Atlantic Ocean. She closed her eyes and took in the smell of the salt and sea. She was relieved to be leaving this place and wanted to put the events of the past few months behind her. She thought things would be different this time, a new place, a new start… but the last year had been a struggle. Too much of her past was trying to catch up with her. As Sophie reflected everything that went wrong, her instincts sharpen and her memories of the past resurface.

She quickly pulls herself together and takes a deep breath as she looks out over the ocean at the sunrise.

Even if moving forward might be worse than this, the longer I stay the greater the danger. The wind was beginning to blow harder and seagulls flew off into the distance. A storm was definitely coming, and even though it was barely autumn, Sophie felt a chill crawl up the back of her neck. This was always a sign that it was time to leave.

"Breathe" by Toni Braxton was playing on the radio as she sped away in her Mercedes. She caught a glimpse of the ocean in the rear-view mirror, and she thought of *him*.

THE END?

About the Author

Catarina's journey began in a quaint town of Monticello, Kentucky where the roots of her Southern charm and culinary prowess were firmly planted. At the age of four, she found herself under the wing of her grandmother, a culinary virtuoso celebrated throughout the town for her exceptional skills in the kitchen. Those early lessons sparked a lifelong passion for cooking and baking that has only intensified over the years.

Venturing into higher education, Catarina pursued her passion for communications and language at college, earning a degree in Journalism and Broadcasting. It was within this realm of writing that she discovered another avenue for self-expression and fell deeply in love with the art of storytelling. Catarina's wanderlust led her to traverse the landscapes of Europe and America, immersing herself in diverse cultures and broadening her understanding of the world. Her affinity for both the written word and the culinary arts converged seamlessly when she embarked on the journey to publish her first cookbook, a culmination of her experiences, skills, and unwavering passion.

Beyond her creative pursuits, Catarina cherishes the joys of life, finding profound fulfillment in her role as a mother. Driven by a desire to share her love for both writing and cooking, she seeks to inspire others to savor the richness of these experiences. Her guiding philosophy, encapsulated in the mantra "Live Well...Eat Right...Find Your Light!" reflects not only her approach to life but also her sincere wish to spread positivity and delight through her words and recipes.

Follow me on Instagram:
https://www.instagram.com/catarinam_author/